RED BOOK

THE
COLOR
OF LIFE

A. L. BASKIN

RED BOOK

THE COLOR OF LIFE

A. L. BASKIN

SBPC

SIMMS BOOKS PUBLISHING CORP.

Publishers Since 2012

Published By Simms Books Publishing

Jonesboro, GA

2023923586

Library of Congress Cataloging in Publication Data

A. L Baskin

"The Color of Love: Red Book

ISBN: 978-1-949433-53-1

Printed in the United States of America

Book Arrangement by Simms Books Publishing

Edited by Safiar Taliaferro

Cover by Urias Brown

Dedication

To my family

And to my mom, Virginia. She always sees something in me that I didn't see in myself.

Thanks for your encouragement and for inspiring me to take this journey.

Table of Contents

INTRODUCTION

Mr. Thompson, my therapist, told me to write. He told me to write down anything I did and how everything made me feel. This book is a collection of my experiences, good, bad or indifferent. It's a combination of daily journal entries, major life events, challenges, and accomplishments. If you look closely, you may find yourself relating to what you find in these pages.

Life is a journey and my life has several colors associated with it. Each color represents a different stage in my life. Each stage has its brilliance and lackluster, but through it all I remain true to myself. Enjoy the journey down the roads that I call *Red* and see where life took me.

CHAPTER ONE

SEEING RED

I was married for twenty-two years and because I was in love, I stayed in the relationship longer than I should have. Love will make you do crazy things. Love will make you make stupid decisions. When you follow your heart, you might leave your family to follow his dreams. Stop hanging out with your friends because he didn't like them. Slash tires when you think he's been cheating. Place a tracker on his car because you don't trust him. Or try to get revenge when you are betrayed. Need I go on?

I really just wanted to love and be loved in return. Alex was the love of my life. We were friends in college before we became lovers and then a couple. Love isn't blind, but love had me with blinders on. Often, we ignore the red flags that are in our face. You can only see the red flags when you are looking for them. So, go ahead and ask the question:

Did I see the red flags? I had chosen someone that graduated from college; had his own apartment; had a car; was gainfully employed as a counselor; had good credit; no criminal record; and most importantly, no baby mama drama or an ex to deal with. I thought I had checked all of the pertinent and right boxes. Conducted a thorough background check.

I was committed to making it work because that's just my personality. I'm an optimist. Failure is not an option because anything can be fixed, including our relationship, right? Wrong. I blame myself. I was wrong for wasting my time. I was wrong for trying to figure out why he wasn't as committed as I was to the relationship. I was wrong for letting my heart get what it wanted.

How I met Alex? Well, that's a story for another day, or should I say another book. I will say that I learned I really didn't know him, even after all those years.

Just like you work out and train your body, you have to condition your brain to recognize the pink flags before they become the red flags that could destroy you, destroy your self-esteem. Before you feel like there's no way out, before you waste precious time on someone that's not worth it, before you do something you'll live to regret, and once you've made up your mind and say enough is enough, it's a wrap.

I was at this place in my life, but Mr. Thompson, my therapist, wanted to be certain I was at that point.

He said, "Today, Mrs. Davidson, I'd like... Mrs. Davidson, are you sure you aren't going back to him?" He had asked me the same question the past couple of sessions.

My response was always the same, "I still love him...but no, I'm not going back to him."

Mr. Thompson didn't know me very well. Honestly, it's

only a small number of people made it into my innermost circle.

At an early age I learned not to trust anyone and still have those scars from that experience. You see, it was my fifth birthday party and my friends and cousins were there. I received many presents that day, however, I mostly received cash gifts. I grew up in a household where you could leave your money anywhere and no one would touch it. I guess someone at the party didn't grow up with the same values and stole the money; someone closest to me betrayed my trust.

As far as that goes, there have been ex-boyfriends who lied to my face when I knew they were cheating; there were so-called friends who stole my idea for a term paper or took all the credit for a college project.

This time was different.

It was Alex, my soon-to-be ex-husband, who had betrayed me after twenty-two years of marriage and having two sons. He was the person closest to me, so it feels more like a knife stab than a paper cut.

So, when Mr. Thompson asked me if I was going back to him, my answer was, "Hell no," and I thought to myself, *Just ask all the other people I've dismissed and am done with.* Their names were like words written on a blackboard. Once the eraser is in my hand and I start to wipe your name from the board, you are erased from my memory. You are booted off the island. You no longer exist to me. I will not let you hurt me again, even if you say, "I'm sorry, please forgive me," or "I'll never do it again." My motto is: "Once a snake, always a snake." And if you've been bitten by a snake once, you don't need to give it a second chance to know it will bite you again. So, Alex can lose my number, just like all the other exes.

Those thoughts made me laugh out loud a little bit and Mr. Thompson asked, "What's so funny?"

I began to tell him this story my pastor shared with us one Sunday morning: It was the dead of winter, and there was this old man in his warm, cozy house. Outside on his front stoop was a snake. The snake was shivering from the cold, looking pitiful, like it was about to die. The old man had compassion for the snake and brought him in from the cold. He nursed the snake back to health. As the man held the snake, it bit him.

The old man asked, "Why did you bite me?"

The snake responded by saying, "You knew I was a snake when you let me in."

Mr. Thompson shook his head a bit as he tried to maintain his composure and said, "Okay Mrs. Davidson, I get the picture. He won't be coming back. However, he will try, once he has been out there and has to start paying for things. He will want to come back to the 'good life.' I just want you to be prepared."

"Prepared? I am prepared. I'm so ready to move on with my life. The shackles have been removed, the blinders lifted, and the taste of freedom has been experienced like a bottle of fine wine. There is no turning back now. I have to be strong and keep moving forward for our sons Kyle and Kobe. Kyle is a sophomore in college in Alabama. He is pretty independent, but still relies on me for a little something-something in his account. Kobe, on the other hand, is thirteen and headed to a new middle school. I'm more concerned about how he will adjust to all the change, since it will impact him more than Kyle."

I knew it then in Mr. Thompson's office, as I know it now; God has revealed that there's much more work for me to do. My life has a purpose and meaning. He will give me the courage to persevere. I closed my eyes and imagined my life without the antics of Alex. There are the fruits of the spirit: joy, passion, peace, and love.

Mr. Thompson interrupted my blissful thoughts with another question. Every time I found a happy-place, he seemed to want to interject something else.

"Mrs. Davidson, can you take me back to the incident that landed you here?"

Suddenly, I felt my eyes swell with tears. Mr. Thompson had thrown me to the wolves. Those wolves nipped and bit at my heels until I was wounded again.

I asked, "Can I rewind the tape a little bit before the incident?" I knew that would help me prepare mentally, physically, and emotionally before I answered his question. And, most important, I'd be able to avoid the avalanche of tears I've been known to generate. Raw emotions are difficult to deal with.

I started my rewind by thinking about Thanksgiving at our house. We usually spent Thanksgiving dinner as a family. It's the one holiday where we could eat and relax without the hassle of driving the long distance back to Ohio.

Thanksgiving had been a special holiday to me in my youth. The patriarchs of the family went hunting and the women would prepare the feast. There were fifty people across three or four generations, all under one roof.

My Uncle Larry Todd and Aunt Mary Liza were splendid hosts. No one else in the family stepped up to host the dinner. After they passed away, it was easier, emotionally, to stay home in Atlanta, where we'd moved from Ohio, than travel back to Ohio for Thanksgiving.

I told Mr. Thompson we were a typical family now living in Atlanta. Thanksgiving and Christmas were my favorite holidays, but this Thanksgiving felt different. Maybe it was the chill in the air; it was hovering around 40°, which is cold for Atlanta. Or maybe it was different because I realized Kyle had turned into a young man before my very eyes.

When he was growing up, I had stressed the importance of education and making good decisions. I had been involved in the PTA and served as a board member for the marching band. I had helped him land his first internship and had taken him to golf practices and tournaments. I was the one at the games when he played in the band, or in the audience for jazz band concerts. This year, he's home from college for the holidays and all grown up.

The one requirement I have for Thanksgiving is that anyone who wants to eat will need to help prepare the dinner. Kobe and Kyle made macaroni and cheese, along with the desserts. I cooked the turkey and made a special stuffed mushroom dish for Alex.

The smells that filled the house were incredible. I probably gained five pounds from the aroma alone. The turkey was golden brown. It was so tender that the meat was falling off the bones. There were also collard greens, my special dressing, and cornbread. I can taste the flavors. The macaroni and cheese was worth every calorie, hot out of the oven and with five different cheeses. The melted mixture was divine.

The dinner looked and tasted wonderful. After we ate, the boys left the house, which allowed Alex and me to have some grown-up time. Our sex life had been sporadic. We went three to six month stretches at a time without having sex, so when he presented the opportunity, I jumped at the chance. It was hard to tell whether he had a medical problem, since he always complained of back pain, or just wasn't interested in making love...at least not with me.

My intuition didn't reveal any clues that he was cheating, but I don't know any man who could go three months, let alone three days, without having sex.

That Thanksgiving night, was different. Alex was attentive and close to his usual self. A couple times before, sex just hadn't packed the same punch and left me even more sexually frustrated. That escapade tided me over as I prepared for my missionary cruise to Honduras, when there would be no husband, no job, no kids (I mean, young men). No responsibility for seven long days and I couldn't wait.

I lay there in bed, letting my mind and body soak in the moment. I didn't know when we'd make love like that again so I ate it up like it was the last cookie in the pack.

After ten minutes went by, my body was still tingling. It had been so long since we'd made love that my body was hovering around ten. Maybe a shower would help soothe my nerve endings. I got up and jumped into the shower. The water pulsating against me was so relaxing; it brought my body's response system back to a manageable five.

When I was finished, I climbed in bed and quickly fell fast asleep. I was later awakened by Alex's movement. He slid closer to me and embraced me. Somehow, parts of the old Alex slowly emerged, as if they were a photograph lying in solution and being developed.

I had seen this before, when one minute things were fine, and the next minute all hell would break loose. I was never sure which Alex I would get at any given time.

Sure enough, it happened the next night. Kyle and Kobe were hanging out at their friend Michael's house. They seem to enjoy spending time together. I kept emphasizing to Kyle the importance of driving and paying attention, because he had to watch out for other drivers. He hadn't been in any trouble; he was "Mr. Cool." He was raised in the church, so he knew how to call on God. He would need that as he went through life.

Mr. Thompson interrupted my rewind saying, "Mrs. Davidson, it sounds like you have done an excellent job raising a wonderful son. You were involved in his activities and laid a good foundation for him."

He paused a second, then asked, "Do you want to talk about what happened the day after Thanksgiving?"

"Yes," I began. "Alex had been smoking marijuana in the garage. I went down there to confront him. When I did, he yelled at me and told me to mind my own damn business. I informed him that anything that went on in this house was my business."

"His eyes were glazed as he towered over me. I told him that I was going to call the police and he dared me to call them. He kept on telling me that I was going to be in more trouble than he was. I didn't know what he meant. I didn't do drugs, I didn't sell drugs, I didn't buy drugs from anyone, but apparently, he had something over my head. I just wasn't sure what it was. So, I dismissed the idea of calling the police."

"His tone was so nasty and abrupt that I felt like I needed more than the cops do defend me. Maybe I should look into getting a 'girlfriend'. One that could fit neatly into my purse and if he tried to step to me the wrong way, well I would have something waiting for his ass. You know, to level the playing field. Maybe I could pick up one this weekend."

I continued speaking to Mr. Thompson, "He slammed the garage door and continued smoking. I went back upstairs and tried to figure out what he was talking about. How could I have been in more trouble? And then it came to me...maybe he planted drugs in my car. If the police came and found the drugs in my car, would I be in trouble? I didn't know the laws on general drug possession. I had to search my car in the morning, and I had to start locking it."

Mr. Thompson explained, "The police may have seen that your husband was under the influence and taken him away. But, on the other hand, depending on what they found in your car, you both may have ended up in jail. It was a tricky move, and I'm not sure of the right answer."

"I'm not sure I did the right thing," I replied, "but, that's neither here nor there. I didn't want to risk anything, since I was planning on going out of the country soon."

Mr. Thompson said, "Sometimes it's good to get away. To let those at home take care of themselves. How was your trip?"

"I had a wonderful time on my cruise. It was a time to relax and reflect. We brought shoes, clothes, toiletry items, and food to feed some of the impoverished in Honduras. Just being able to help someone else is truly gratifying."

"When I got back to the states, it was almost Christmas. When you go to a warmer climate, it makes you forget that it's December. Wearing shorts and sandals takes your mind off coats and boots."

"After I returned, me and the boys prepared to go to Ohio for Christmas—one of Kobe's favorite traditions. I bring all of the fresh seafood for Christmas Eve, and then we have a traditional Christmas dinner. We invited Alex, but as usual he declined. It was either too far of a drive, us not staying long enough, him not wanting to stay with my family, him not having anything to eat, or him not having the time off or enough money. "

"He had a million and one excuses to stay in Georgia but I wasn't going to let that dampen our spirits. So, we headed to Ohio without him."

I went on, "Kyle offered to help me drive. I knew I-75 like the back of my own hand, and I've driven it by myself with the boys on numerous occasions. However, I indulged him. Kyle couldn't stay awake long enough to get out of the state of Georgia, so I knew he wasn't going to be driving the entire trip."

Mr. Thompson asked, "Why do you think your husband didn't want to join you on this trip?"

"That was one of Alex's typical responses," I replied. "He never wanted to vacation with us. He always had a lame excuse. This was probably all bullshit and maybe one of the flags I missed. He would have three to four days to do whatever the hell he wanted to without my knowledge or presence. We have been on vacation without him to New York four times, New Jersey three times, Florida five times, Texas three times, and Ohio twenty times. I always intended to make sure that the boys were able to go to different places to see what the world looked like outside of Georgia."

"The drive to Ohio was more meaningful this time around than ever. My grandmother, who was ninety-four at the time, wasn't doing very well. I had surprised her and my mother with a quick trip in October, being that I didn't know how much time my grandmother had left. She was the one person in my family who stressed the importance of having a relationship with God. When we were growing up, she took us to church and told us to trust in the Lord."

"I always thought I inherited some of her characteristics, such as cold hands. That being said, I loved and admired my grandmother dearly. She was a vibrant, God-fearing woman who cut her own grass, climbed the ladder to fix her own roof. She had always been self-sufficient. She didn't ask anyone for anything."

So, he could get a true picture of her, I told Mr. Thompson, "Grandmother was light brown in complexion, with flowing gray hair. She was 5'7", and she knew the Bible inside and out. She grew up with a large family. I think she was one of ten, and at the time, she was the last living out of the ten."

The thought of losing her made tears well up in my eyes. I quickly wiped them away before Mr. Thompson could catch on. I needed to be strong.

"You have inherited some great qualities from your grandmother," he said, "your trust and belief in God, tenacity, self-reliance, independence, and love for family. Now, what you are going to need to do is develop a love of self."

I wasn't sure what he meant at the time. I thought I loved myself. I treated my body like a temple: no drugs, no smoking, and no tattoos. I also worked out occasionally, ate right, and got enough sleep. I've completed college, maintained a career, and I take very good care of myself. *Why did he say I need to develop a love of self?*

I suppose Mr. Thompson spotted the inquisitive look on my face and decided to elaborate, saying, "Mrs. Davidson, what I mean is that you have done so much for others with your time and sacrifice that you need to put yourself first."

Put myself first. I let those words resonate in my head.

"Put myself first," I said aloud. "You know, as a wife and mother, you tend to want to make sure everyone's needs are met. Yours often get pushed to the back burner, to another day, another year, or never. It may take me some time to get used to this ranking order..."

CHAPTER TWO

OHIO

We arrived in Ohio ahead of the big storm. The boys always prayed for snow on Christmas and in Ohio you had a much better chance of having that prayer answered. Mom greeted us at the door and we unloaded the Lexus. With food and gifts in hand, I quickly asked her about Grandma.

You see, Mom thought it was best to move Grandma from Georgia to Ohio about seven years ago. Back then, there wasn't anyone close to Grandma in Georgia. There was no one to check on her. Of course, Grandma fought it tooth and nail every step of the way. However, we did what was best for her.

"She's been sleeping a lot," my mother replied. "She doesn't want to eat, and she's had trouble walking."

I gave her a great big hug and told her that she had done a wonderful job taking care of Grandma.

"The old lady doesn't appreciate it," Mom said. "If it were left up to her, she would have been dead.

But she can't go until God calls her home."

I reassured my mom that Grandma was grateful for all she had done, even though she didn't express it.

"I know it's hard doing something for someone, taking care of someone and buying food for someone who doesn't have the decency to say thank you. I know the feeling all too well. It makes you feel like you're being taken advantage of. But, at the end of the day, you could tell yourself that you did all you could do, and go on with peace of mind. Otherwise, it would make you bitter and resentful, and that's not where you want to be. Your mom took care of you when you couldn't, and now you are repaying the favor."

We embraced again before I headed upstairs to visit Grandma. For whatever reason, Grandma seemed to listen to me more than she did to Mom. Maybe it's that generational thing, or maybe it's because I was the favorite. Yes, I said it; I was the start of the next generation, the first grandchild. I was the favorite, and everyone wanted to imitate me. Good thing I set a very high standard for them to follow.

Grandma was in her room, sound asleep in her bed. I knocked on the door and entered the room, saying, "Granny, it's time to wake up. There's no sleeping while I'm here."

Her room was dark. The shades and curtains were drawn. I stepped in and peered at her. She'd lost some of her brilliant cocoa color; it had been replaced by a darker ash color. Her bed had sucked all of her strength into the very mattress that used to support her. Her eyes slowly opened up. They had a dull, blue tint to them. It appeared as if she had been on a journey, a million miles away, and that she had struggled to come back. She finally realized that it was me standing in the room.

"Mia," she said in a low voice.

"Yes, we're here. And, it's time for you to get up."

Her bed was piled with a blue blanket, a white blanket, a beautiful multi-colored blanket, a quilt, and two large comforters. It was as if she was buried underneath the covers. She seemed to spring to life as I removed layer after layer. She sat up and hugged me. We talked for a while. She then asked about the boys. I told her they were downstairs. Next, she asked about Alex.

All of my family asked about him, but he never asked about them. It's ironic that my ailing grandmother was still concerned about someone else, instead of being focused on her own health. She asked me to give him her love. I nodded in response.

My goal that Christmas had been to help Mom with Grandma, even if it required me to cook, clean, or organize things. That was my mission. Also, Mom needed a break, so I told her she could leave, and that I'd stay with Grandma.

It had to be difficult working and taking care of someone you love. My sister Brianna helped out during the evening and they had a caretaker that had proven to be unreliable. I wished there was more I could do.

On Christmas Day, we exchanged gifts. Grandma decided to come downstairs. She had eaten her breakfast, got clean and fresh, and was ready for the day.

"She is just showing out because you're here," Brianna said.

"Well, I'm glad she's up and about, but I'm not sure I can come back every weekend," I responded. We shared a laugh.

The next day was filled with shopping. We headed to the mall and hopped on the after Christmas bargains.

Chris drove us over to the Half-Price Book Store. While there, Kyle recommended that I get *50 Shades of Grey* to read before the movie came out. *50 Shades* caused me to feel warm all over. There were so many sexual acts. I got so hot every time I picked the book up.

A day or two later, we left Ohio. It was difficult, because I wasn't sure if the next visit would be for Grandma's funeral. I didn't want to think about it. We took pictures with Grandma as we left. Before our departure, I leaned down and kissed her on the forehead. After we finished packing the car, we left to return to Georgia.

CHAPTER THREE

THE USUAL SUSPECT

It was 5:30 a.m. The traffic was light, and the cops weren't out yet. Therefore, we cruised through the dark highways. We were already in Tennessee as the sun started to rise. The miles melted away like butter. The boys were quiet and I suppose they were just ready to get home. We made it home in record time, without any incidents.

Alex was home and waiting for our arrival. We ate, drank, and got it on until the break of dawn. I put *50 Shades* to use. The next night was a repeat performance. I was on vacation from work, so I was able to make love all night and then sleep in.

Later, Alex showed me a picture of a vibrator and then said, "You might want to get you one of these." At the time, I thought he was looking for some new sex toys to spice up our sex life. Needless to say, my interest peaked. He also agreed to buy me some books. That rarely happened and I started to wonder, *what's really going on?*

I told Mr. Thompson about Christmas and our return to Atlanta, *and* about Alex's sexual attention. But I also said I knew things were too good to last.

Alex returned to his usual self after New Year's when he wanted me to buy a mouth guard for Kyle. He texted me all the specifics since he had done all the research. "Kyle has sleep apnea. That's why he is snoring. You should use your HSA monies to buy him a mouth guard for him to use while he's sleeping". He just needed me to write the check. I refused and texted him "First, has Kyle been diagnosed with sleep apnea? No, he hasn't. He's not overweight. In fact, he's an athlete. You don't know what you're talking about. But, if you think this mouth guard is so important, then you can pay for it yourself. Kyle is in college and he's not gonna wear that stupid looking device."

"Everything blew up from there. When I got home, Alex began ranting and raving about how I had thousands and thousands of dollars in my bank account. He asked why I wouldn't pay for the mouth guard and again I told him I wasn't buying it. I walked to Kyle's room and Alex pursued me, so I just left his room."

"As he followed me down the hallway to our bedroom he shouted, You selfish bitch! I can't believe you won't spend $60 damn dollars on your son!"

I was so irritated that I turned and yelled back, "You're working now. He's your son, too. Buy it your damn self. I get tired of you telling me what to spend my money on. Stay out of my face."

"I twirled, walked to the master bedroom, and slammed the door in his face. This didn't deter Alex. He entered the room anyway. I did my best to tune him out, but his voice was loud and abrupt, as if something was going to happen to me if I didn't buy the mouth guard."

Mr. Thompson asked, "Were you afraid that he would get physical?"

"Yes," I replied. "He was so angry. He only saw me as a checkbook. The way he was in my face, I was really afraid and he did all of this in front of the boys. It was devastating. I felt humiliated and totally disrespected.

"After all of that, Alex moved into the guest bedroom. That was probably the best move because I was so enraged, I might have used a baseball bat on his reconstructed back so he could see how that felt. I just prayed for relief."

I continued, "No one should have to put up with that but I didn't see a way out. What kind of an example was he setting for the boys? And he calls himself a Muslim. What Muslim man doesn't take care of their family? Yeah, he adheres to some of the doctrine, you know, no pork and praying to Allah. But being a provider, being a leader, he must not have read those surahs. I should report him to the Fruits of Islam and have them deal with him. Maybe they will revoke his Muslim card."

I told Mr. Thompson that between Alex's outbursts, continued drug use, and offensive behavior, I knew it was over for good this time. I could feel the love leave as if it were being sucked right out of the air. I deserved better, to be treated better.

Meanwhile, as I told Mr. Thompson, Kyle was set to head back to college. I told him to stay focused, make us proud, and not worry about what's going on in Atlanta. We were going to be fine.

He felt bad about leaving Kobe behind to face the situation alone. I assured him that Kobe would be ok since school was starting in a couple of days.

I continued with my story, telling Mr. Thompson that on January 5th, as I was preparing for work, Alex casually walked into the bathroom and said, "Mia, I don't love you anymore. I haven't loved you for several years and I'm moving out of the house."

He said this so nonchalantly, like he had been plotting his exit for more than a couple of months and wanted to gauge my reaction. A mix of emotions flooded my mind... joy, relief, anger, resentment, and happiness. All of those emotions were followed by the deafening sound that prevents you from hearing anything else that a person says.

Despite hearing Alex's announcement, I knew God had finally answered my prayer of release, so I know He has provision stored up for me. I took my marriage vows seriously, even the 'till death do us part.' We had been in a loveless marriage for such a long time that I thought God had forgotten about my prayer.

I must have been in shock, because all I could do was nod my head at Alex. When he finished, he politely left the bathroom, walked back down the hallway to the guest bedroom, and climbed back into the bed. There was no discussion about his decision.

I thought to myself when I came to my senses, "What the hell?" I became extremely angry. All the times I wanted him gone and now he gets to pick when he leaves. "Why don't you get your ass up now and pack your shit? Better yet, I'll help you pack, I yelled from our bedroom. Proceeding to the bedroom walk-in closet, I started to politely throw his clothes off the rack an onto the floor. Too bad I don't smoke or it would have been a *Waiting to Exhale* moment. The next option was to throw them out the window onto the lawn, but I couldn't open the window.

Alex jumped out of bed and came storming into the master bedroom.

"What the hell are you doing with my clothes?"

"You better be glad all I did was throw them on the floor," I said waving a wooden hanger in his face. This was all I could get my hands on at the time. "Now get the hell out of my bedroom. No, as a matter of fact, get your ass out of my house," as I pointed the hanger in the direction of the door.

Alex decided it was probably best that he leave and headed back to the other bedroom.

I was so upset with Alex; my blood pressure was up and tears were streaming down my face as I continued to get dressed for work. I can't explain why I was so angry. I was expecting him to move, I just didn't know when. This was something I had prayed for and it got answered. I think it was the fact that he was leaving on his terms, but wouldn't leave when I had asked him to. I felt totally rejected and lacked control over the situation.

Since Alex seems to like the element of surprise. I had a surprise for him. Before I left the house, I asked him, "So, do you want to file for legal separation, or divorce?" I must have caught him off guard with that question. He stared back at me blankly, as if he couldn't believe I was moving to that step so quickly.

He hesitated, but eventually said, "Whichever you prefer."

I left for work, but I couldn't concentrate with so much going on in my mind.

Mr. Thompson asked me, "Were you worried about making it on your own?"

Maybe I hadn't shared it with him, or maybe he simply forgot, but I paid all the household bills. Alex didn't do shit. Financially, I knew I'd be able to make it on my own. I'd done it for the past fifteen years. I imagined that it wouldn't be much different going forward.

Alex wasn't worried about taking care of the house, so there were a few things that needed repair. And there were things I just didn't know how to do, or couldn't reach, or was never taught... No, I'd still be better on my own than in my current state.

"I'll manage, I've been taking care of everything anyway," I replied to Mr. Thompson, "however, there was something puzzling about Alex's decision and the timing of it just didn't sit right with me. I was still upset, but determined to know, why now? Alex was so cunning, I felt like a beetle trapped in a spider's web. He had lured me with unforgettable love making in December to walking out the door in January. I needed answers."

Later that night, when Alex was asleep on the sofa in the family room, you know what I did? I checked his damn phone for text messages and phone calls. Nothing. There is always a reason for their reaction and I was determined to find out what it was. There were no red flags with him staying out late or hanging out on the weekends. He couldn't afford a romantic getaway and his job as a claims customer service rep, didn't come with company travel perks.

Next, you know what I did? I went through his briefcase. Men always leave a trail, some piece of clothing that smells like perfume, a receipt for dinner, texts, and I'm a bloodhound hot on his trail. I wasn't going to stop until I found something.

I searched for clues, evidence to support my gut feeling that something didn't add up. How did he get enough money to move? Was he moving in with somebody? What are we going to tell the boys? Call it women's intuition or call it just a hunch, but my snooping did pay off. Eventually, I found his notes from a chat with an individual, a female. There, he stated his likes and dislikes, and that he had two boys. And of course, he forgot to mention that he was married.

As I continued reading the document, he stated that he liked music and was digging her vibe but when he gets bored, he's gone.

What the hell? I couldn't believe the words that were on the page, so I read them once more. Needless to say, a whole flurry of emotions ran through my body. I could feel the anger rising up in me like the flame on the stove. How long had he been playing me? Taking advantage of my kindness?

I recalled to Mr. Thompson that I began to think, *evidence, I must gather evidence.* Those were the thoughts in my head. *This is the very proof you need to make him pay. He must have a blog. Everyone is sharing and posting their business on Facebook or some other social media outlet.*

I wondered if he had a blog about yoga or back strengthening. Maybe back surgery? How to cheat on an unsuspecting spouse? Whatever the case, I slowly crept down to the basement, careful to avoid the loud, creaky steps as I descended. I didn't want to wake anyone in my quest. It was still cold down there. I walked over to the printer and copied the two pages of raw cheating. Now, where to hide them?

"I slipped his notebook back into his briefcase and then stuffed the copies into my backpack, alongside my work papers. Next, I went into the garage and took photos of his drug paraphernalia and marijuana that was in his car. There was this aching feeling in my body. You know, like if you were stabbed in the heart. It was the pain of betrayal."

"That must have been devastating," Mr. Thompson said. "You were a loyal spouse. It's not easy to forgive someone who broke the marriage vows and stepped outside the marriage. You can muster the strength to go forward. You are valuable, and if Alex didn't see it in you, there will be someone else who will."

I took solace in knowing that moving Alex out opened the door for the one who would love me for who I was.

Alex thought he was smart, slick, a true player, however, now that I knew his trump card, I was at ease. At that moment, I really just wanted him out of my life, out of my house. *He's already wasted too many of my precious years with his back and forth. Let me just pray for him and send him packing,* I told myself.

"Mr. Thompson, you don't know what it feels like to be trapped in a loveless marriage. To have your husband acting as a roommate. To constantly go through the motions of being married. Deceiving your family to put up appearances. Maybe I should have just left everything and moved on. Maybe I should have cheated on him since I wasn't getting the love I needed at home.

His excuses for not wearing his wedding ring are so *he could get more clients and he didn't want to damage it when he worked out at the gym.* That was a clear red flag that I missed. He no longer wanted to be married. I made him wear his ring whenever we went out together and when we made love. This was my way of having him respect the marriage, even if he was halfway out the door.

"Mrs. Davidson, I can't say that I know what it's like to be in a roommate marriage, but I know it must have been difficult keeping up a facade, by appearing to be in a happily married relationship. This would take a toll on anybody and having an affair wouldn't have solved anything. It is just like being in an abusive relationship."

I paused for a minute. "You're right. I never looked at it that way. It felt like a mentally abusive situation. I was bitter and angry and I just wanted out."

That night, I bagged up his clothes in black garbage bags and left them in the garage. That way he wouldn't have far to go to get his shit. I wish it had been garbage day so I could sit his clothes on the curb.

When he came home, he asked why did I put his things out and started playing a game about feelings. He stated that I never expressed my true feelings. This was another one of his manipulative tactics. I explained that I was as transparent as I could be. In fact, I helped you pack so you can get the hell up out of my house. I refused to entertain his foolishness, his attempt to blame me for the failed marriage, to climb back onto his merry-go-round ride, just going around in circles and repeating the same cycles. I could see through the bullshit because I had the evidence folded up among the papers in my backpack. This was a game of poker and I wasn't going to show my hand.

Inside, I was saying to myself, *"I got you right where I want you. Dumb ass. Now I just need to find out who she is."* On the outside, I kept my blank face so he couldn't read my next move.

Instead of leaving like I had hoped, Alex went upstairs to the guest bedroom.

CHAPTER FOUR

INCIDENT

I've always prided myself on being calm and even tempered. I think what really pushed me over the edge was the feeling of being used and betrayed. Just the other day, we had made our peace. We were both ready to move on. I prayed for him and I finally got the release that I so desperately desired. It took a lot out of me to allow someone who clearly didn't love me anymore to continue to live under my roof. Brave or foolish, I allowed our relationship to continue beyond the point of return.

He doesn't love me and he made this fact known through his controlling actions, abrupt behavior, his selfishness, and his lack of care or concern. My once *baby* transformed into my worst enemy. He allowed hatred, envy, jealousy, and bitterness to control his every move, like a puppet on a string.

I continued telling my story to Mr. Thompson by saying, "It was Wednesday morning. After I dropped Kobe off at school, I decided to work from home. Something in my gut made me question Alex's every move, his every motive. Something just didn't add up and I was determined to find out what."

"As I worked in the downstairs office, I could hear the sound of running water. *This is my chance*, I thought to myself. I had already uncovered him writing a blog to a female, indicating that he had two sons, liked music, and wanted to get to know her. Persistence Pays Off was written at the top of the page. He concluded that page with saying that he was available anytime.

"How ironic; all of the things he never wanted to do with me or never had the money for, he's *now* able to spend time and money on someone else. Oh, and in his blog, he never mentioned that he was married. As if I didn't exist."

Mr. Thompson interjected, "This was probably one of the most difficult ways of learning that your spouse was unfaithful." He added, "Do you think there were other signs, other than not wearing his wedding ring?"

"Yes, I'm sure of all the times he turned me away, or couldn't get it up. He definitely had a lack of interest, but these were the first real pieces of evidence. I placed a copy of that letter in my backpack, too."

Mr. Thompson commented, "I know you aren't going to like the next question, but can you tell me how this made you feel?"

"I felt betrayed, but at least that gave me the answer to his behavior. I liked the explanation and closure. I had both. I didn't have to guess or pretend. I could move on. No more playing house or listening to his ranting and raving. I had the upper hand, because he wasn't aware that I knew his secret. I could strategize my next move. Playing chess is better than playing checkers."

"I continued working, but since I could still hear the shower water, I had this uncontrollable urge to see what else he had been up to. I decided to check his phone to find out who *she* was. I quickly moved from the office like a cheetah to ensure my window of opportunity. His cell phone was usually locked by a passcode. This time, the phone was there for the taking. I grabbed it and checked his emails first. Nothing. Next, I moved to phone calls. Nothing again.

"Then I moved on to text messages. That's usually the easiest way to communicate. I let my fingers scroll through the standard exchanges between him and his family. There was nothing out of the ordinary there. His sister mentioned that he could take the boys to the doctor, that it wasn't always my responsibility. *True that!* I agreed. There were some exchanges between what appeared to be co-workers, a drug transaction between him and Kenny Parker, who was selling medical marijuana for $40. I remember thinking, '*Wow! He had money to spend on weed, but couldn't pay a bill at the house, ridiculous!*'

"I started to give up and put the phone down, that is, until I discovered an exchange between Alex and Suzanne Banks. They chatted as if they were getting to know each other. She lived in Kennesaw, and they were making plans, now get this, to hike in the mountains up there on Saturday. How convenient."

I continued, "On Monday, he told me he was moving out after being in a loveless marriage, then Saturday he is hiking with Suzanne. I was furious, to say the least. What the hell? A sea of emotions from betrayal, anger, being taken advantage of, hurt, '38 hot,' as my girlfriends would have said. I had never felt that way before. I paced around the house with the phone in my hand, the very phone I paid the bill for. All the bullshit that I endured with him. All of his controlling, outrageous requests. All of his *I love you's* on cue, but didn't mean any of it. All this took me to a dark place deep in the pit of my soul. I was devastated at my core."

"I remembered all of the times he was sick and I nursed him back to health. How I stood by his side when he told me he wanted a divorce seven years ago, but didn't have a place to go and asked if he could stay at the house to save money."

Having to recall that day and tell Mr. Thompson was so difficult, but I continued, "Who in their right mind would do such a thing? Who would allow themselves to be rejected, neglected, and abused in this manner? I considered myself a strong, smart, educated woman, but who does this?"

"Now this was the ultimate sting in the face. I could feel the blood boiling in my veins. There's a thin line between love and hate as the song says and I had crossed over. I hated feeling used and that's what he'd done. He'd stolen my time. What a waste. Time I'd never get back. That was wasted on someone I thought loved me. I felt like a fool. I wanted to get even. I wanted him to feel the pain that I felt in the moment. I found myself wandering around the garage. I felt the desire to smash something, to destroy something, to let go of the pain that I had been holding inside for ten years. I needed a release valve and I found it in the form of a hammer."

"What could I do with a hammer? Smash his car windows? Better yet, let him feel the pain I felt by smashing his phone in front of him. That would keep him from contacting that bitch."

"He was out of the shower when I entered the room with the hammer in one hand and the phone in the other. As he stood at the sink, I approached him with a look of pure, uncensored hate. I twirled the hammer in my hand as I moved closer, but kept the phone tucked behind my back."

I said, "You must think I'm a damn fool." First, he simply gazed at me through the reflection in the mirror. Then he saw the hammer in my hand and his eyes quickly widened, as if he were a deer caught in headlights."

I advanced further into the bathroom. "Who is she?" I asked. He never had a pot to piss in before he met me. He stammered, "I don't know what you're talking about."

I told Mr. Thompson what happened next by saying to Alex, "Don't play dumb with me. Who have you been talking to, texting, blogging, and emailing?"

Alex stated, "Nobody." I yelled, "Liar!" Then I leapt from where I stood and lunged toward him. I wanted to take his head off with the hammer. It would either knock some sense into him, knock him out, or leave a permanent mark and he would never forget *Mia* when he looked in the mirror. My anger and adrenaline let me get two well deserved blows to the head and two to the chest. I wanted to kick his ass. At this point, I realized that I had miscalculated things, just a bit. The major issue was that he was 6'0", 210 pounds and I was 5'3", 135 pounds.

"He anticipated my every move from then on. This made me even more furious. He quickly grabbed me by the wrists and twirled me around like a ballerina across the stage. The phone flew out of my hand and glided across the floor, landing under the base of the cabinet. We danced this magical dance and slid onto the rug in front of the tub."

"'Let go of my hands!" I screamed.

"Let go of the hammer!" He yelled back at me. He lifted me up off the floor, both of our hands were still locked around the handle of the hammer, and we continued the dance and then barreled out of the bathroom into the bedroom.

"Let me go!" I screamed. As he proceeded to bear down on me from behind, the towel dropped to the floor and I told him I was going to stomp him in his nuts. He tried to clamber down, I tried to break free.

"I'm sure you can guess who won the battle. He slammed me down on the floor, face down, and proceeded to put his knee in my back; he stretched my left arm out as I lay with the hammer in my right hand under my windpipe. I asked, "Who is she, who have you been fucking?"

He said, "No one, only you."

"Liar!" I responded and he leaned in on me more and more. I told him to get off of me.

"I can't breathe, I can't breathe!" He insisted that I let go of the hammer which was lodged between the floor, my windpipe, and 210 pounds of pressure. I released my grip on the hammer. He slid it from under me and slowly got up off of me. I started coughing and gasping for air. The tears flowed as I asked, "What's her name?" All I wanted was for him to admit to the name Suzanne that I saw on his phone. He kept stating that he didn't know what I was talking about. Deny, deny, deny was his stance.

"You tried to kill me," I told him. "I couldn't breathe and you didn't get up. Get away from me." I was sobbing uncontrollably as I asked him again, "Who have you been fucking?" He tried to console me by holding my arms.

Alex responded, "Nobody." He finally released me and I ran out of the room. I found myself pacing the floor in the office downstairs, and then sat at my desk. I was shaking, almost trembling, thinking, *I can't believe this shit.* "Get out of my fucking house!" I yelled at the top of my lungs.

I could hear movement above my head, but I didn't hear any footsteps coming down the stairs. After 30 minutes, I got up from my office chair.

He saw me coming back up the stairs, locked the bedroom door, and barricaded himself inside. He kept insisting that he didn't know what I was talking about. I banged on the door and asked him to tell me her name. I went back downstairs and continued working.

After another 30 minutes, I came back up and stated, "Tick-tock. You are going to have to leave soon to go to work."

Then there was a knock at the front door and Alex yelled from the bedroom, "The police are here." The person who never wants to involve authorities has called the police instead of simply leaving the house.

"Mr. Thompson, I don't feel comfortable talking about anything else related to the incident. I've never had someone call the police on me. Just suffice it to say that he lied; I was questioned, and then arrested. The bitch ass stood there gloating at the top of the stairs as I was dragged out of the house in handcuffs."

"I understand, Mrs. Davidson. Would you feel comfortable talking about what happened after you were released?"

"I literally cried from the time they handcuffed me until I was in the intake area. I had never been confronted by the police and there were five of them, all males, at my house. I felt outnumbered. That no one understood my position, no one heard the pain, and no one felt my suffering. They were there to do a job and I was the end result of it, not a victim, but a quota. The police officer tried to assure me that everything was going to be alright. His words fell on deaf ears. My life was over. Everything that I had worked for, everything that I had strived to become was washed away like footprints in the sand once the tide had rolled in. I cried so much that my eyes were red and puffy and I kept repeating, 'He wants to get me fired.' I was inconsolable in the back of the police cruiser. I didn't do anything and yet they arrested me. The officer told me I would be out that afternoon. I ended up spending the night in jail because there wasn't a judge to set the bond. I had left a slimy mess of tears and snot in the backseat of the cruiser. I apologized for the mess."

CHAPTER FIVE

RELEASED

"Mr. Thompson, I'd like to skip my incarceration details because, as you know, that's why I'm here speaking with you."

"Ok, Mrs. Davidson. Some of your experiences have been painful and hard to deal with."

"Yes, I survived the night. Everyone on the inside was helpful. I went to court the next morning and bail was set. Things were looking up. Alex could have bailed me out and I would've made my one o'clock meeting and no one would be the wiser. Yet, when I placed the call to Alex, he said he didn't have the money to bail me out. In fact, he seemed delighted that I was released, but still behind bars. We did a 3-way call with Pastor Steve, who said he would do it. Alex also said that when I got out, he didn't want me to contact Kobe. I thought to myself, *What? Kobe is my baby (although he is 13 years old). Why is he doing this? Why is he trying to keep me from my child? Why is he going out of his way to hurt me?* He wanted to leave the marriage and now he wants to destroy me. This time I cried on the inside."

"It took all day for the bail process to be completed. I was released and Pastor Steve picked me up. I can never say how much I appreciate Pastor and Lady Elect. We don't have family in Georgia, so it's good to know that there are some people in your corner. Pastor shook his head in disbelief.

He said, "Sister Davidson. I didn't think you had it in you."

I said, "I didn't either, Pastor."

"I thanked him for paying the bond and he stated that he didn't. They went to the bail bonds place to pay and was informed that it was already taken care of. We continued to drive to my house. I tried calling Alex but he didn't answer. I wasn't sure if he was at the house or if he left the door unlocked."

Pastor looked at me and said, "I know you love him, but he doesn't love you. You need to let it go."

I took a deep breath and replied, "I know. He hasn't loved me for several years now. He stopped wearing his wedding ring about seven years ago which should have been an indication that he didn't want to be married anymore. And after this incident, it's really over."

"Baby, baby, when he told me he was too busy with getting his things to pick you up, I knew something was wrong," Pastor said.

"Yeah, he was planning on moving out, so I hope he's not at the house."

I told Mr. Thompson that Pastor tried to reach Alex. It was around 9:00 p.m. and slightly mild for a January evening. This time Alex answered and said he was busy and should be there in 45 minutes. We proceeded to the house. I was drained physically, emotionally and spiritually. God has to be in the plan. I was tired, hungry, scared, and just wanted to sleep. We pulled up to the house.

We were still trying to figure out how the bail was posted when Brianna called. She asked if I was home and that they were coming down. I briefly shared with her that I had been locked up, to which she replied, "I know. I spoke with Kobe who was crying and traumatized and he told me you were in jail. I posted your bail."

Oh my, I was shocked. I was trying to keep the family out of my issue. But now it looked like they are involved. I couldn't thank her enough. The cavalry was coming. I have to go back to the bail bonds place where Brianna posted the bail; Pastor and I had gone to the wrong place. Brianna said they needed more information and I wanted to stay out of jail.

Pastor and I waited for Alex. I didn't have any keys. I was able to put the code in to open the garage, but I didn't have keys to the house. I checked the car, no keys. As we waited in Pastor's car, I called for a resource officer. I didn't want any more incidents. It was getting colder and later. I just wanted to sleep in my bed. The officer arrives and asked what happened. I told him it was a domestic dispute and I would feel comfortable with someone being at the house.

Alex finally pulled up in a huff, like we had disturbed him. He didn't speak to anyone, unlocked the door and asked the officer a couple of questions and then whisked off like the evil witch from the Wizard of Oz.

Everyone agreed that it was probably not safe for me to stay at the house alone. The house was in complete disarray. *Good, he's moving out,* I thought. I scrambled to find some clothes. The house seemed foreign to me. A flood of memories hit, of good times, but mostly of Alex yelling at me or telling me I needed to pay for something. I finished packing and headed out. Off to the bail bonds place and then the hotel. It was close to midnight before I settled into my home away from home. I'd go to the office Thursday, tomorrow, and keep everything hush-hush.

CHAPTER SIX

THE CAVALRY

The family arrived Friday afternoon and we stayed at a different hotel closer to the house. They were in disbelief. I begged them not to come, especially since Grandma wasn't feeling very well, but they pressed on. We had dinner together. The next day, I started the process of finding an attorney.

Kobe had orientation at the School for the Arts. Alex didn't want me there but allowed me to come if I sat away from him. Auntie Brianna and Kobe shared a photo with their matching hats before Alex insisted that Kobe leave.

The family wanted to see Kobe, but Alex had plans for him all weekend. We finally caught up with him at the house. Alex tried to be slick as we sat in the minivan on the side street watching the lights go on and off from room to room as they tried to rush out of the house.

Alex had made Kobe help him move things out of the house. That's why Kobe wasn't available. He was determined not to let the family see Kobe, but as he opened the garage to leave, Auntie was standing in the driveway. Alex didn't have a choice, but to let Kobe go with her to the minivan. Kobe got hugs from my mother, whom he called Nannie, and from Auntie and DJ, my nephew. He took a picture with Grandma and Nannie gave him some spending money. Everyone was glad to see him, even if it was only for a couple of minutes.

Mom said, "He's going to do everything to hurt you, stay strong." I nodded in agreement. The family left to go back to Ohio on Sunday, and based on Alex wanting to have access to the house, I packed more clothes and decided to stay at the hotel to avoid any more conflict and confusion.

In my counseling session, I said, "Things were looking up. In fact, Mr. Thompson, your sessions have helped me face some of my deepest issues."

"Such as?" Mr. Thompson asked.

"Well, acknowledging my own self-worth and loving myself. I tended to put everyone's needs above my own."

"Very good," replied Mr. Thompson.

CHAPTER SEVEN

TEMPORARY

Work is work. Life was getting back to normal, except I hadn't been able to see Kobe. Alex had moved Kobe in with him and wouldn't share the location. Alex sent me a series of text messages.

"Mia, did you tell the people at work that you were arrested? They should have never let you out of jail. You're gonna lose your job over this."

I tried to ignore his threat. Then the worst possible thing happened.

I was in a meeting with JoAnne, my supervisor and some other vendor partners. When Natasha interrupted the meeting, JoAnne stepped out, and then she came back in to get me and escorted me to a conference room. In the room was a police officer. I felt like I was going to faint. I hadn't violated any terms of my bail, hadn't seen Kobe, and hadn't prevented Alex from taking things from the house. I told myself, *I was trying to avoid as much conflict as possible. Now Alex was just being an asshole. Why was this happening to me?*

The officer presented me with a temporary restraining order. I was so embarrassed, humiliated and devastated. No contact with Kobe, a request for custody and spousal support. I needed a good attorney, and fast. Oh, and I wasn't to touch his things which were strewn around the house. I signed the agreement and staggered back to my desk. I felt like I'd been punched in the gut and was gasping for air.

JoAnne asked, "Are you ok?"

I replied, "My husband just filed papers." I couldn't share with her that it was really a temporary restraining order.

I know God has not forgotten me, but why must I endure such deep emotional blows? This was such a lonely, dark place. I don't know how I'm going to get through it.

All of that happened between my weekly counseling sessions, so at my next session with Mr. Thompson I explained what had happened the past week and asked if he knew an attorney that can handle a TPO and custody battle. He put me in touch with Ms. Walker.

Our consultation went well. She was on point. We were getting prepared to go to war. As Romans 8:31 states, "If God be for us, then who can be against us?" How dare Alex try to take Kobe from me?

Alex's dad called me. I didn't want to answer, but we've always had a good relationship. He apologized for Alex's behavior and said he was glad I didn't hit him.

"I don't know what he told you, but I didn't try to hit him, I tried to smash his phone," I stated.

"Do you have an attorney?" he asked.

I replied, "It's just a hearing and my momma didn't raise a fool."

He was working for the other side, trying to extract information. Well not from me, not this time. How could he have raised such an uncaring, controlling, manipulative, narcissistic person? Fruit doesn't fall far from the tree, so he either got it from his mother or father.

We went to the war room at the attorney's office. I thought of Isaiah 54:17: "No weapon formed against me shall prosper and every tongue that rises up thou shall condemn." We reviewed the final details. I told her Pastor and Lady Elect would be there as character witnesses. We were ready for battle, suited up, prayed up, and taking no prisoners. I could barely sleep the night before.

I was not familiar with the court system. I tried to stay on the legal side of the law. Brianna called me in the morning to reassure me. I made my way to the courthouse.

CHAPTER EIGHT

WELCOME TO
HOLLYWOOD

Lights! Camera! Action! That's how I would describe Alex's behavior in court. He served me with a temporary restraining order and we were at the hearing. My attorney had suggested that I hire a court reporter to get a transcript of the proceedings. This was a smart move in case I needed to use Mr. Davidson's testimony against him. The court reporter walked in and introduced herself and went to set up.

I sat with my attorney. Pastor and Lady Elect were there if we needed them. I was dressed very professionally. My attorney thought Alex would agree to working out an arrangement. I told her, no, he wants a hearing.

Lights: He entered the courtroom in jeans, his blue polo shirt, and a green jacket that was 10 years old. He looked weak, broke, and beat down. He was by himself, no attorney. That seemed odd, since he was requesting alimony, child support, and custody. Brianna warned me that he would pull out all the stops.

Camera: He looked pitiful, like a victim. Maybe he thought this would help his case, since he was in fear of his life. This was a bitch ass move. He didn't have a pot to piss in since I was no longer his financial backer. He tried to look frail and destitute so he would be awarded alimony, to be a *kept man*. Please, he needed to find another job or reduce his expenses.

Action: As he walked by me to take the stand, he quivered, as if he was afraid of what I might do. The court appointed attorney asked him some basic questions about his interaction with Kobe, his parenting, etc. Alex started by talking about the incident with the hammer and said that was why he left with Kobe.

Oh, I couldn't wait for the cross examination. There were so many inconsistencies in what he stated. Attorney Walker drilled him about his work schedule. It was 12:30 pm to 8:30 pm, which didn't allow for much interaction with Kobe. If this had been baseball, strike one!

"Who makes the decisions for medical care and who covers the children on insurance?" Ms. Walker asked Alex.

"I do." Strike two!

Lastly, he tried to infer that I was crazy and needed professional help, adding that the incident was unprovoked. My attorney referred to the text messaging and blog to another woman. Strike three! He's out!

What really made everyone in the courtroom take notice was the fact that he was disrespectful to my attorney and requested that she apologize to him. The nerve of him. My attorney presented evidence of drug use and Alex said he didn't take the picture; he never admitted to marijuana use or the contents of the bag in the picture.

Alex ranted, "I already answered your question, now apologize."

The judge had his head in his hands and just shook his head. He finally asked if there was a pending case, to which my attorney said, "Yes."

The judge said, "Case dismissed."

I was elated! Relief swept through my body and the beauty of it all is that we had it transcribed. Alex scurried out of the courtroom, or should I say slithered like a snake in disgust. He was sure he was going to win and be awarded money to sit on his ass. Not this time. "To God be the glory; great things He has done," as the song goes.

My attorney and I exchanged hugs and headed out of the courtroom. "Attorney Walker, I can't thank you enough. Now that the TPO case is over, I still have to deal with the assault charge. Do you know a good attorney?"

"Mrs. Davidson, you're welcome. Yes, contact Attorney Tonya Coleman at Coleman and Coleman Associates. Tell her I referred you."

"Thanks, again."

"Sure, we'll talk soon."

I had to wait for the judge to sign the dismissal paperwork. I walked into the hallway and told Pastor and Lady Elect that the case was dismissed and I thanked them for coming.

Pastor said, "One of the court deputies came out shaking her head."

"Yeah, he was a piece of work in there. He had the nerve to ask my attorney to apologize to him. I guess he didn't realize that I would get a copy of the transcript."

We all laughed. How ludicrous! A lady in the courtroom said that I should have knocked some sense into him.

I got the official court paperwork and left to go to work. Victory felt good, but how long would it last? I really wanted to get back to some sort of normal. At least I had an attorney for the other case; I'll reach out to her tomorrow.

Life was so different; maybe that would become normal. I hoped Kobe wasn't traumatized. Why would Alex try to drive a wedge between me and Kobe? Didn't he realize we were inseparable?

We spent the first night catching up. It seemed like the couple of weeks we'd been apart were like years. Kyle probably knew what was happening because he and Kobe were so close, but I tried to keep Kyle out of the court proceedings as much as possible.

CHAPTER NINE

REINFORCEMENT

They always say you need the phone number to an accountant, to keep your money safe; a pastor to keep your soul in check; and a good attorney to keep you out of jail. I had two of the three areas covered, but I didn't have a good criminal attorney. Why would I need one? I hadn't been in trouble before, so there was no need to have an attorney in my contacts. I had some down time so I took the opportunity to contact Attorney Coleman.

"Hello, this is Attorney Coleman. How can I help you?"

"Hi, Attorney Coleman. My name is Mia Davidson, Attorney Walker referred me. I'm looking for an attorney to work on my assault charge."

"Mrs. Davidson, I'll need to get some information about the charge. Can you come to the office around 4:30?"

I quickly checked my calendar and replied, "Yes, I can."

Attorney Coleman's office was a couple of blocks from my office which made it extremely convenient. I just hope she agrees to take my case. God will fight your battles, but I need an attorney that can persuade the judge. Her office was on the 50th floor of the building with a magnificent view of the Kennesaw Mountains.

I arrived around 4:15 and the receptionist escorted me to a conference room down the hall. Attorney Coleman walks in. She is a tall, beautiful, caramel colored woman with long black hair. She looked like she could have been a model.

Attorney Coleman extended her hand "Hi Mrs. Davidson, how are you doing?"

I shook her hand. "Hello Attorney Coleman, I'm doing well."

"I was able to pull the police report, court documents and I'm waiting on the 911 transcript to create your file. I go to bat for my clients because I believe everyone deserves a second chance, that's what God's grace is about."

This confirmed it for me. This sealed the deal. She was definitely the right attorney to handle my case. The cavalry had come earlier and now I've gotten reinforcement.

"There are some details that need to be addressed. Can you explain what happened? And whatever you share will be covered by attorney-client privilege which means it can't be used against you."

I was a little hesitant at first, ashamed of my actions, but felt justified in what I did. From how see it, he had it coming to him and got just what he deserved. I took a deep breath. How many times will I have to tell this story, to relive the trauma, to admit I lost control, to share the consequences of my actions to disclose the regret I felt for being arrested? This time was different. I didn't have the tears that I had when Mr. Thompson asked me to recount what happened. You know, the INCIDENT. Attorney Coleman was someone that could actually get me out of serving time in jail. So I knew I had to give it to her straight. She had probably heard worst cases than mine.

"Attorney Coleman, I let my emotions, my anger and rage get the best of me when I found out that my husband of 22 years was not only moving out, but that he was seeing another woman. They were going hiking and doing things that he never asked me to do. They had been texting and when I saw the message, I just lost it. "

"I wanted him to experience the pain in my heart that I felt at that very moment and the only way I thought of was to make him feel the same pain. So, I grabbed a hammer, walked up to the master bathroom and proceeded to hit him with it. I know my pain was more emotional than physical, but I wanted to physically hurt him, to beat his ass. I'm not a psycho, but every time I think about it, I'm not sorry for what I did because I think he deserved it. I am sorry that I didn't take the iPad he used to message his brother to call the police. He barricaded himself in the bedroom, waited for the police to arrive, pretended to be a victim and had me arrested. I didn't think he would call the police because we were fighting. I've been working with my therapist, Mr. Thompson on my anger issues and being able to express myself. There was so much resentment bottled up inside that it exploded like a ticking time bomb."

"Was Mr. Davidson injured as a result of the altercation?"

"No, he may have had a few red marks where I hit him with the hammer, but nothing serious."

"Mrs. Davidson, the police have charged you with assault. Has Mr. Davidson moved out and have you filed for divorce?"

"Yes, he moved out the same day I was released, but I haven't filed for divorce. There was a TPO case that was just dismissed, so I hadn't thought about filing for divorce. Also, since he was the one that wanted out of the marriage, I figured he should be the one to file."

"Were there any witnesses to the incident?"

"No, I had taken our son to school that morning, so it was just the two of us at home. I worked from home that day. He should have just left like I asked him to. It really seemed like a set up. Like he was getting advice from someone on how to work the system. *Bitch ass*. Filing a TPO was really unnecessary because he was out of the house and our son wasn't there when the incident happened."

"Attorney Coleman said that without any witnesses, then it's his word against your word, which gives us a good chance. I'll present you with all of the options that we have after we have our first hearing. I want to hear what evidence they have. I'm familiar with people in the DA's office so I'll check with them on how they are proceeding with the case."

"I know sometimes we get caught in situations that we really didn't mean to be in. I understand how you felt after being betrayed by Mr. Davidson after 22 years of marriage. It must have been devastating. I think under the circumstances that it was an "in the heat of the moment" reaction. I can tell that it was totally out of character for you. While I'm checking into when the hearing will be scheduled, start making a list of individuals that can be character witnesses or can write a statement on your behalf. Someone other than a family member."

"Also, make sure you don't have any encounters with Mr. Davidson. Always have another person with you are someone on the phone with you when dealing with Mr. Davidson. And no encounters with the police, including any traffic violations. I need you to be a model citizen until your case is resolved."

I laughed inside. I wanted nothing to do with him, so I had no problems steering clear of him. I nodded in agreement.

As Attorney Coleman escorted me out of the office, I final felt a sense of relief, like I had someone that understood me, who had my best interests in mind, and most importantly, who would fight for me to keep me out of jail.

"Thank you, Attorney Coleman."

"Thank you, Mrs. Davidson. I'll email you the paperwork and we'll be in touch in a couple of weeks."

CHAPTER TEN

WHY?

Mr. Thompson said, "May I ask a different question, Mrs. Davidson?"

"Sure," I replied.

"Why did you stay with Mr. Davidson?"

"Why? Why? I don't know. There were a myriad of reasons, excuses more like."

"Let's discuss the most relevant," Mr. Thompson said.

I began, "It was so hard to think about. Every time I think of why, I feel like such a fool. Why didn't I see the clues? Why wasn't I more tuned in? Why did I allow him to treat me like that? Why wasn't I stronger? Why did I think this was love? Why did I let it get to this place? Why didn't someone help me see the light? Why didn't I notice the red flags that were right in front of my face? Why would I blame others? This was my mistake. Why was I deceived?"

"The first reason I stayed," I continued, "was because I thought the boys deserved both parents in the same house, no matter what. Alex always seemed angry about his parent's divorce; divorce runs in his family and I wanted to keep the family intact."

As I talked with Mr. Thompson, I was thinking that I had been married for so long I wasn't even sure how to start looking for another mate. The game had changed so much. How do I meet new people? I don't even have a Facebook profile. What's the saying about knowing the devil you are with?

I said, "I stayed because I didn't think anyone else would be interested in me. I was committed to Alex, not flirting with other men."

As I continued talking, I did some soul searching on the why. I went all the way back to my childhood. When we were growing up, my dad always threatened to leave but never did. Then he was diagnosed with cancer and died within two years.

I told Mr. Thompson, "I think my brain equated leaving with death. If Alex left, he was going to die. I know it sounds silly, but I think that was the main reason I stayed. I was hoping that one day he would realize I was not the enemy, but his friend. I was hoping that he would genuinely love me one day, that he would not be manipulative or cunning. And I was hoping that I could last until both boys were in college but fell four years short."

"I hate that life will be different for Kobe, back and forth between two households, two different parenting styles and expectations. I've failed him and I'm not sure how to right the wrong for him."

"Mrs. Davidson, it's not uncommon to try to find a correlation between events, to try to take control of situations and to want to live a happy life. But there isn't a reason to believe that death would be a result of him leaving. I think you realize that you can't keep someone that doesn't want to stay. Some of your *whys* have made you a stronger individual. Only God knows why things happen the way they do. Take this experience as a life lesson and move onto the next level."

Who would have thought that my *why* could inspire me to get closer to God and let him lead.

All I could say was, "Thank you, Mr. Thompson."

CHAPTER ELEVEN

PAPERS

I'm working from home today to get caught up. I've got to call and get funeral information. My grandma wasn't doing so well and Mom isn't going to make any decisions. I hope I can finalize some things so I'll be prepared to pay a portion of the funeral expenses.

The doorbell rang. I'm not expecting anyone or a delivery. I answered the door.

"Yes, may I help you?"

"Are you Mia Davidson?" the man asked.

"Who wants to know?"

"Are you her?" he asked.

"Yes," I responded reluctantly.

He then handed me an envelope and said "You've been served."

I closed the door. Now what? I slowly opened the envelope and started to read. The sting of the words on the official document took me by surprise. Alex has officially filed for a divorce. One would have expected some conversation, but not from him. He was into "shock and awe," not "sit and talk things over." Still, the words on the page were cold, final.

I read through the document. Of course, he wanted spousal support and child support. This was too much to handle. I walked upstairs and started crying. I'm glad no one is home to see me like this. I think I just need an emotional release, just to let it all go.

God did give me the release I prayed for; I just needed to let it all go now. So much had been stored up inside as I attempted to stay strong. This was another lonely dark place for me. God wouldn't put more on me than I could bear, but this was a heavy load.

CHAPTER TWELVE

ANGRY BIRDS

Over the weekend, we were exchanging emails between the attorneys. We had an agreement, with just a few changes. I can't believe he wanted to do a 50/50 split. I could live with that as long as I'm primary for Kobe. Maybe his attorney was able to talk some sense into him.

I arrived at court at 8:30 in the morning. I wanted to make sure I was on time. I saw his attorney, but Alex wasn't in sight. My attorney was going to be late because of a time conflict. The courtroom door opened about 8:50. Still no Alex. We entered the courtroom; there are about eight cases on the docket and we were the first case.

I sat on the front row. It was 9:00 a.m. and the judge wasn't on the bench. Alex arrived about 9:05. His attorney acknowledged his arrival with a slight nod. He sat in the back of the courtroom. This time he was dressed in a blue and white print shirt, khaki pants and brown shoes; this time he didn't appear desolate.

We had an agreement, except for the taxes. The judge passed over our case as Alex's attorney indicated that my attorney was going to be about 45 minutes late. My attorney entered the courtroom about 9:20. I briefed her on what happened. The two attorneys stepped outside.

When she came back in, my attorney said, "We are close, but Alex doesn't want to agree to the taxes." I explained that we had to agree because they needed to be refiled. They had Alex and I discuss the taxes in the hallway.

"I don't know what's up with your tax people. They are just idiots. They didn't send me the link," Alex clamored.

"They said they sent it on April 21st," I replied.

"I'll take care of it today," Alex stated.

He was so angry. I wasn't quite sure what he was angry about. He was paying summer camp fees instead of child support. He got off easy. I'm not the one to take his last penny.

I told him, "You were supposed to take care of it a long time ago."

"I said I'll call them today," Alex yelled as he went back into the courtroom.

My attorney came back out. I told her that I wanted the taxes added to the agreement, primary custody, exclusive use of the marital home, return of keys, and taxes uploaded to the tax preparer.

She conferred with his attorney. He finally agreed and his attorney modified the document. I walked up and down the hallway until she came back with the final version. I reviewed it and added vision coverage.

She then asked, "Do you two talk?"

I replied, "Not so much. I think he hates women. Successful women."

We waited for the judge to sign the documents. His attorney asked Alex if I could walk down with them to get a copy of the documents. I strutted down the hall with Alex trailing behind. I knew I was looking good with my heels and shapely legs. We got the copies. I thanked his attorney and left the building.

I couldn't believe he would give me temporary custody. He had some type of trick up his sleeve.

"How is your relationship with your sons?" asked Mr. Thompson.

I replied, "My sons love me, but Alex has a way of making me the 'bad guy' while he is their 'buddy'. He's very defensive. He acts like it's a competition between us. Like the boys are punished, seen as weak or wrong for loving their mother. Alex never corrects them if they disrespect me."

"It is unfortunate that he's raising them to be disrespectful to you and other women. I'm afraid they may pick up some very bad habits," Mr. Thompson stated.

"I should've picked up on how he treated his own mother. He would barely call her and resented her for helping his older brother. He would only see her if there was a large family gathering. Now that I think about it, I can't ever remember him saying let's take a trip to Texas to see her. He wasn't very close to her. I thought it was the physical distance they had, but now I think it was the emotional distance they had. This was definitely a red flag that I missed."

"Mrs. Davidson, the relationship that a man has with his mother is important in determining the relationship he will have with other women. And this is often overlooked."

Now someone tells me, I thought to myself.

CHAPTER THIRTEEN

STAY WITH THE LORD

Winning the temporary custody case felt like things were coming together like the pieces of a jigsaw puzzle. Our lives had been scattered in so many directions. This was a victory and time to celebrate. That was until mom called.

"Mia, I hate to bother you because I know you have a lot on your plate."

"Mom, what is it? Is everyone, ok?" There was an award silent pause. As if mom didn't know how to bring herself to say what was on her mind.

"I wanted to let you know that Grandma is in the hospital. Can you speak with the doctor?"

My heart sank. I had been tied up with the court case and hadn't been able to travel to Ohio to see Grandma. Now she's in the hospital. "Sure, mom. I can talk to the doctor." Mom handed the phone to the doctor.

"Hello, this is Dr. Cohen. I want to be honest with you so that you can make the best decision for your grandmother. She has stage 4 ovarian cancer, low blood count, and is very weak. There's nothing that we can do to treat her condition."

I tried to hold back my tears as the doctor explained there was nothing he could do. "How much time does she have?"

"It's hard to say, but probably less than 6 months."

I began to weep when I heard how much time she had. I had hoped to be able to see her, but between work and the court cases, I'm not sure I'll be able to get away.

"We'd like to move her to hospice and make her as comfortable as we can. We need your permission to give her some blood to build up her strength before we move her."

"Yes, please give her a blood transfusion. What type of facility are you transferring her to?"

"We'll transfer her to Kennedy Rehab Central. They have a great hospice unit within the facility. I think she would be more receptive if you explained it to her."

I reached for a tissue to dry my eyes and thought about what I was going to tell grandma. I didn't want to lie to her, but I didn't want to give her some false hope. She was 94 years old and had lived a long, wonderful life. She was the last sibling out of ten.

I was the oldest grandchild and of course her favorite. It wasn't a secret. Don't get me wrong, she treated us all the same, but I held a special place in her heart. She trusted me with her *personal business* and access to her bank accounts. We had a great relationship. She really loved her family and if it wasn't for her, I probably wouldn't have a relationship with God. In fact, one of her favorite sayings was, "Whatever you do, stay with the Lord." This resonated with me throughout my life. I tried to live and do what God directed. She was also a prayer warrior so I thought I would say a quick prayer before explaining where she was going. I know she wants to go home, but this would not be the case.

"Grandma, how are you feeling?"

"Mia, I'm tired and just want to go home."

"I spoke to the doctor and he said you are tired because you blood count is low. If you let them give you a blood transfusion, you'll have more energy." They need to transfer you to a rehab facility where you can gain your strength. Once you get your strength up, they'll let you go home."

"If you think that's best, Mia."

"I do think this is best for you. Can you please hand the phone back to the doctor?"

"Dr. Cohen, she has agreed to the blood transfusion and the transfer to the rehab center."

"Thank you, Mrs. Davidson. We'll start the procedure right away."

I felt content with the decision I had made, but cried about it. I never made it back up to Ohio to see my grandmother. I was able to wish her a Happy Mother's Day via FaceTime. She passed away at the end of May and I was able to help pay for the services. She was laid to rest next to the love of her life, Pete in Trimble, Georgia.

CHAPTER FOURTEEN

SUMMERTIME

The summer was a blur. Even though they split their time between our two households, the boys stayed with me most of the time. They were glad to be together and that helped them cope with everything.

I was still grieving the loss of my grandmother and hadn't had a chance to really take care of myself, but at least there was no unexpected paperwork delivered to my work or doorstep.

I avoided Alex at all costs but wondered if everything was a lie, some type of deception. I should have noticed the clues. I found myself feeling empty trying to find meaning in it all. I didn't want to burden Brianna with the details, but I needed to get it out of my head. This was a very difficult journey and I didn't know when it would end. I just had to take one day at a time.

When school started, Kobe was mad because I took his Xbox so he decided to stay with his father. This was a very welcomed change, because before Alex couldn't or wouldn't take them to school. At least with Kobe over there, Alex was spending money on clothes and school supplies. I knew this was too good to be true.

Alex would try to use it against me that he was taking Kobe to school, but I finally got a break from taking him and picking him up. All Alex wanted to do was prove that Kobe spent more time with him so that he could be primary. I could see right through this tactic. I just wished I didn't have to scrutinize every action, every inaction, every move and gesture. I couldn't afford any missteps. Everything that was said or done had meaning that was compounded. I couldn't let my guard down. I needed this process to be over.

He always wanted me to buy something or pay for something but I didn't owe him anything. At times, I wished he would just go away. Just go be happy with the life he had chosen. Didn't he understand that he couldn't tell me what to do or how to do it anymore?

The month of October was such a blur. We were busy at work, where I'm a project manager for a Fortune 500 company in Atlanta.

There was so much to do in so little time. I was so tired and don't have the bandwidth to deal with Alex. He was supposed to file the taxes back in August, but when I called the IRS, my SSN was not in the system. He had lied yet again.

I had come to believe the opposite of whatever he said. The truth wasn't in him and I would never trust him again. His intent was to ruin me. Most people like and respect me, but I'd never experienced pure hatred from someone I was married to for 22 years. You'd think you would know a person by then.

Since he didn't file the taxes, I was scrambling to get it taken care of. I emailed Attorney Walker and told her I didn't believe Alex had filed the taxes. I then contacted Dennis, the CPA. After Alex bullied me into sending him all of my tax information, he didn't do what he said he would. The good news was, Dennis had my tax information and I told him to proceed with the filing.

Attorney Walker called and said, "Hi, Mrs. Davidson. Mr. Davidson has left us with no option but to file contempt. He will not learn until he has to pay court costs and attorney fees."

No, he probably wouldn't learn unless it had to do with money. Now, I was stuck with paying the taxes and late fees for believing that he would do the right thing. I prayed that all of this money would be returned to me.

CHAPTER FIFTEEN

SLAYING THE
DRAGON

2015. This year is almost over. It was the end of October. The leaves were turning their vibrant yellow, red, and orange. The weather turned cool for a couple of days, so the house felt damp. Sometimes, I welcomed the quiet, but other times it was a reminder of what life used to be, when the boys would be laughing and playing, there was the smell of food cooking on the stove, and the warmth of family. With Kyle at college and Kobe with Alex, it all felt different.

At times, I screamed, "FREEDOM," from the top of my lungs. Other times, I cried in the shower to wash away my tears. At other times I had to keep telling myself that I had done everything for someone who didn't appreciate it, so now I was doing it for myself.

I was not used to the loneliness, the lack of intimacy. It had been almost a year since I'd made love or had any affection. I needed someone to tell me it would be alright.

That someone was my mom. She listened to me and encouraged me. She told me I'd get through this. I'm strong and resilient.

Work was going well. Teammates seemed to like the new look of the communication materials and this should lead to a sizeable bonus. I asked myself, *Why didn't Alex try to better himself instead of looking for me to take care of him?*

I could feel an argument coming on because Alex kept asking for money. This time, it was to pay for Kobe's drum lesson. I spoke to Derrick, the drum instructor, and paid $140 in cash when I took Kobe to his lesson on Sunday. I didn't mind paying for it, but it was the way Alex asked. No, he didn't even ask, he basically demanded that I pay because he didn't have any money.

Alex also kept asking about tutoring for Kobe but hadn't offered any money. So, I set up sessions with the tutor, Mr. Copeland, for Tuesdays and Wednesdays. After his Wednesday session, I dropped Kobe off at Alex's and headed home but decided to stop by the grocery store first.

As I was driving, I noticed that Alex was calling me. *How did he get my new number? What does he want?* It was cloudy and dark. I saw that he left a message and decided I'd check it when I got home. I hopped out and ran into the store. The phone rang again and it was Alex. I'd decided to call him when I got home, but the phone rang again. I answered it.

Alex immediately ranted, "Where is my money? Pay me what you owe me. Kobe doesn't have any food."

I responded, "I don't owe you a damn thing. You need to provide for Kobe when he's with you, just like I take care of Kobe when he's with me."

Alex continued, "You owe me for school supplies. You are a trifling deadbeat. You are a sorry excuse for a mother."

I explained that I bought school supplies, school clothes, his suit, and took him to get a haircut.

"Liar," he said. He continued with his rant.

I asked, "Is there anything else regarding Kobe?"

Alex continued, "You are a selfish deadbeat. You don't give a damn about your kids." He then cussed me out and stated, "How will it feel when you lose your job?"

Crazy. First, he wants me to pay him and now he wants me to lose my job. Well, I just ignored him and responded, "If there's nothing else concerning Kobe, then I'm going to discontinue our call and don't call me with your bullshit." I hung up.

He called me back like a stalker. I didn't answer. It would be pointless.

Later that evening, I checked my emails. Alex had sent a couple of emails and voicemails. *What was his problem today?* I logged on to my work computer. He had sent the same message to my work email: "YOU OWE ME MONEY!

PAY ME MY MONEY! This was uncalled for. I never sent emails to his job. I was furious. *What was he trying to prove? He acted like a bitch ass.*

Thursday morning, I responded to his email, telling him to consult his attorney and not to send emails to my job. In turn, he fired off another email to my work email address. I contacted my attorney and forwarded her the string of emails from Alex. Attorney Walker said that Alex would stop harassing me with his request for money and that I didn't owe him anything. In fact, Mr. Davidson was in contempt for not filing the taxes jointly. Not only would Alex be responsible for attorney fees, but for sanctions and restraining orders, too.

Attorney Walker slayed the dragon and caused Alex's eyes to bulge as she held the sword in her hand to cut off his head. No more fire-breathing dragon to deal with. I was glad there was someone that could put him in his place. I did my happy dance. He couldn't say anything to the attorney or be disrespectful to her again. I could only imagine what he was saying to himself: "Who does she think she is? I will F*** her up! She doesn't know who she's dealing with!"

What is his next move? I asked myself. Maybe he'll go somewhere and sit down. At least for now the threat of being in contempt has the dragon slayed. *I wonder what made him hate me so much.*

He wanted a divorce. I didn't contest it but granted it. He should be ecstatic, but he appeared to be wallowing in pure hate. When I emailed him, he didn't respond, but when he needed something, I was supposed to drop everything. I told myself, *I don't frustrated that I haven't had to ask him for anything. Not one damn thing.*

I'd come to realize that I was doing it on my own anyway, even when he was here, so it really didn't make a difference.

Sometimes, when he was spewing his venom of hate, Kobe was in the room. I kept praying that Kobe didn't pick up any bad habits. I really wanted him to learn how to respect women. Alex should just be a man and move on.

CHAPTER SIXTEEN

THANK*SELFING*

This year was almost over and now it's the week of Thanksgiving. I told Kobe that I wasn't cooking Thanksgiving dinner. He just looked at me like, "Really?" His facial expression said that I shouldn't deprive him of the tradition, even though our family dynamic had changed.

Kobe asked, "Is Kyle coming?"

"Yes," I said. "He called and said he'd be home Wednesday."

I relented and spent a couple of days preparing the food. On Wednesday, the boys helped prepare and asked what time we were having dinner the next day. I said around 4 o'clock. Then they stated that Mr. Rob, Alex's lifelong friend, had invited them over.

Really? Really? This was Alex's doing. We had always spent Thanksgiving together; it had been my favorite holiday. This year, even though I'd decided I wasn't cooking, I changed my mind for the boys. I wasn't going to let him ruin this day for me or them.

Instead of being upset, I told them, "Fine. You can go." I continued preparing the meal while listening to gospel music. They got dressed and left the house. Inside, I felt really empty, but we prayed before they left.

I told myself, *I'm not going to be depressed.* I was going to turn it into Thank*selfing* and do something for myself, by myself. I decided to go to the movies and do some Black Friday shopping. It wasn't ideal, but it would take my mind off the pain for a couple of hours and show them that I'm not always home and available to them.

****

Kyle was preparing to go back to college. These days have flown by and I don't think that I had a chance to really check-in with the oldest. He was sitting in the office at the computer. I walked in and he asked, "Mom, how are you doing?"

I replied, "Kyle, I'm fine. Dad and I have some paperwork to complete, but other than that I'm good. I need you to check on Kobe to make sure he's ok."

"I will, Mom." Kyle stated.

"So, how are you doing?" I asked Kyle. "Let's check those grades."

"Hey, Mom, Nicole isn't coming back to school. She decided to go home to do hair."

Inside, I was elated. We had been praying that he would find a different girlfriend. Not that I had met her, but she didn't seem to have anything in common with him except going to the same college. This was his first true girlfriend in every sense, and it was hard to break that tie. Prayer had moved her out of the state, if not totally out of the picture.

"Oh, Kyle, you know sometimes you have to follow your passion if it's something that you're good at and you can make money."

"Yes, she's good at doing hair and wanted to start making money."

"How are you feeling? We can have you talk to someone when you come back in December. Sometimes it helps to have a neutral person to talk to."

"Yeah, Mom, I'd like that."

He pulled up his grades and I noticed an F in computer science.

I said, "Kyle, that can't be correct."

"Mom, let me explain. All of the grades aren't in yet. I should end with a B."

"Ok, Kyle, that's what I expect to happen."

CHAPTER SEVENTEEN

BON VOYAGE

I couldn't believe I was leaving for my missionary trip in three days. Where had the time gone? I packed my bags and supplies for my second trip to Honduras; printed out my tickets and grabbed my passport Brianna would be joining me this time and I was looking forward to seeing her. I needed this chance to get away from the pressures of the job, scrutiny of the courts, and mostly Alex's request for money and food. I'd have no contact with any of them. I really needed this me time. Sometimes I felt like I was under a microscope or wearing a scarlet letter. It seemed like everyone knew what I did; no matter how much I tried to hide it or pretend it didn't exist; it reared its ugly head.

We were in the embarkation line ready to board the boat and we'd been in a line that stretched two miles. Finally, it was my turn. The agent asked for our paperwork and passport. I politely handed them over. She scanned my passport and I didn't hear the all too familiar "ding." She smiled and tried again. Yet again, nothing. I looked around; no one else was having this problem. Why me? She politely stepped away and went to a desk in the corner and talked to two officers. My heart was pounding and I was starting to sweat.

Brianna and I exchanged questionable glances. What was the problem? My order didn't say I couldn't travel. Oh, no. What if I spent all of this money, only to find out I was not supposed to leave the country? *What am I going to do?*

The three agents were still talking and we were holding up the line. I felt like everyone was watching me. I nervously looked around, thinking, *any moment, there will be several police to haul me off.* I began to say a prayer silently.

A few more minutes passed and the agent returned. She apologized for the delay, handed me back my passport and took my picture for the room key. I breathed a sigh of relief. I could continue with my missionary trip. As we walked toward the ship, I still kept looking over my shoulder as if someone was coming to get me, but no one came.

****

"Hi, Mr. Thompson, did you miss me last week?"

"Well, Mrs. Davidson. Yes, I did and I must say you look well-rested."

"I had an amazing time. We fed 90 families in Honduras and took over 100 pairs of shoes. We ministered to the people. They were so thankful and appreciated the small things. We are so blessed in the USA and really don't appreciate it. It was such a humbling experience for me."

"I'm glad you had a wonderful time and were able to give back," said Mr. Thompson.

"It's all about helping others," I replied.

"So, how are you feeling today?" asked Mr. Thompson.

"I feel okay. I'm planning to go to Ohio for Christmas. I can't believe this year is almost over. In some respects, it seemed like it crawled like a snail and other times flew like the wings of a hummingbird. Other times it was suspended. This was the most difficult and challenging year of my life. It can only get better from here."

CHAPTER EIGHTEEN

HOME FOR THE HOLIDAYS

As I prepared to go home to Ohio, Kyle and Kobe decided to stay in Atlanta. I wasn't surprised; I expected it. I told them I'd go without them and set out on Christmas Eve. My car could practically drive itself to Ohio since I'd done it so many times.

The rain was coming down in buckets, at times making the lines in the road extremely hard to see. I cruised at 75 mph, no cars and great music. I told myself Christmas would be different without the boys, but I was not going to let that dampen my spirits. The rainy weather already tried to do that. This time driving alone, allowed me to kick back and sing along with my favorite artists. Just me and my angels.

Brianna had warned me that mom's house was going to require some attention; it was just my nephew DJ and her so it couldn't be that bad. Boy, was I wrong.

CHAPTER NINETEEN

BLATTODEA HAVE
TAKEN OVER

My mom likes nice things and doesn't care to throw away things even after they have served their purpose. She tended to hold on to EVERYTHING. I could almost characterize her as a hoarder. Maybe it came from her upbringing when she treasured everything. Whatever the case, I was not prepared for what I saw when I reached the door.

I could barely open the door without stepping over shoes and boxes of clothes stored in one corner of the hallway. A chair blocked the furnace vent in the hallway. There were papers everywhere, clothes everywhere. Mismatched pieces of furniture were scattered throughout the living room. My mom has some great qualities, but throwing out things is not one of them.

Brianna had to prepare me for the worst part. Mom also had an army of Blattodea – cockroaches -- that had taken over her kitchen. Where did one begin? I can't stand cockroaches and they were everywhere... under the stove, crawling in the cabinet, scurrying across the kitchen backsplash, and peeking from underneath the refrigerator. I hate roaches. Let me say it again, I hate roaches! I get sick just thinking about them. I left my suitcase in the car. I didn't want any of them hitching a free ride to Atlanta.

We started by clearing out the discarded furniture in the hallway to make a path to the other rooms. I started just chucking stuff in garbage bags. It didn't matter if it was old or new, working or not. These things had to go. Then we moved on to the living room to gather the papers for Mom to review and determine what could be thrown out. DJ took the clothes up to her room.

By the time we got to the kitchen, I was exhausted. I felt like I needed to put on some combat gear to protect myself from the roaches. I got the creeps thinking about them scurrying around, let alone actually seeing them! It was worse than I thought. This was going to be war. I grabbed a pair of gloves, a garbage bag and bug spray, and started tossing food from the cabinets into the garbage bag. Once the cabinets were clear, we moved the smaller cabinet out into the hallway and then started sweeping, mopping, and spraying. There were momma, daddy and baby Blattodea running everywhere. They all had to be killed if we were cooking Christmas dinner here.

It took us three hours to get the kitchen under control. We set out traps to catch those we didn't see. This was not how I had planned on spending my Christmas. After we finished with the kitchen, we moved on to the living room and dining room. I was totally exhausted; it was past 9:00 p.m. before the house was in decent shape. This was going to be Mom's Christmas gift from us.

That night I couldn't sleep and tossed and turned, just imagining all of the Blattodea that were in the kitchen. I knew we did a good job, but I kept wondering what if there were still some hiding in the walls and what eggs could hatch later. I couldn't see myself staying, cooking, let alone eating there.

When I got to Brianna's, first I made an appointment for the exterminator to come out to Mom's. This situation required the professionals. Second, I made reservations at the Montgomery Inn for us to have Christmas dinner. This was definitely a Christmas to remember, or should I say forget.

CHAPTER TWENTY

PULL UP YOUR BIG
GIRL PANTIES

Attorney Walker had sent me an email with "Final Hearing" in the subject line. I was expecting mediation. Why are we going to a final hearing? I was truly taken by surprise. There was a lot to prepare, more documents, more statements, more and more information. What happened to mediation? I was hoping we could talk things out, but that seemed impossible now. Attorney Walker wanted me to come to the office the next day.

I felt like I was 9 months pregnant, due any day, with swollen feet and a big belly filled with an alien of a new life moving and kicking in me. I couldn't wait until this divorce baby was born. It had been almost a year. Who carried a baby for 12 months? Zebras? Monkeys? I'd have to google that. I gathered the hospital bag full of documents and waddled to the attorney's office.

"Good afternoon, Attorney Walker."

"Hello Mrs. Davidson, come on back. As I stated in the email, we are preparing for the final hearing."

"Yes, but weren't we going through the mediation process?" I asked.

"We initially thought that we would try it, however, Mr. Davidson's counsel asked to be removed."

If he hadn't listened to her on filing the taxes, he surely wouldn't have listened to her on any custody discussions. "It would be a waste of our time," stated Attorney Walker. I nodded and agreed and then we got down to strategizing.

"You want to retain custody, marital house, and your retirement assets?"

"Yes, that's correct," I replied.

"Mr. Davidson says Kobe signed some papers?" Attorney Walker asked.

"He said he didn't. Kobe likes the flexibility of going between the two houses."

"Can you bring him to my office on Sunday?"

"Sure, I can do that."

I waddled out of the office. I thought it would be pretty easy to trick Kobe into going to the attorney's office, but he would tell Alex where we were going. Alex manipulated Kobe and he reported back every action and every statement I made. How was this going to work?

I decided we should see the attorney right after Kobe's drum lesson. Kobe didn't go to church with me on Sundays, he stayed at Alex's. Think, think. I told myself I'd pick up Kobe, which would feel normal to him, and after the drum lesson we drove toward home. The attorney's office was near the house, but Kobe would have texted our location to Alex.

We passed our street and Kobe asked, "Where are we going?"

I quickly changed the subject, asking, "Why did you miss church?" He said he played at a church inside a theater. Interesting.

We pulled up to Attorney Walker's office and hopped out. It was cold and windy that night. We exchanged introductions and then the two of them headed back to her office.

Tomorrow was the big day. I could barely get any sleep. The divorce baby would be delivered in the morning. Everything was ready for it. I said my prayers and went to bed.

CHAPTER
TWENTY-ONE

MR. GREEN

I arrived at the courthouse around 8:40 am. After going through security, I headed to the 6th floor. The doors to the "delivery room" opened at 9:00 sharp. I selected a seat on the front row of the courtroom. Attorney Walker came in and sat by me. We conversed before the judge entered. Alex had already arrived, but his attorney wasn't there yet. There was a young black man looking like he was right out of high school that entered. I'll call him Mr. Green. He walked over and sat by Alex. I wondered who he was.

The judge came in and started the calendar call. When she came to our name, we both stood with our attorneys. Attorney Walker wasn't familiar with Mr. Green so she approached him to see if he wanted to discuss the case and come to an agreement. They left the courtroom to converse down the hall and I was left there, listening to other cases and occasionally having the court reporter glance at me.

After what seemed like an eternity, but was probably more like 45 minutes, my attorney came back in the courtroom and motioned for me to leave. We tried to find a private place to talk, but all the rooms were taken. We decided to go to the 5th floor; it was quiet down there and we grabbed a bench to discuss options.

I told her once again that I wanted to pursue primary custody and I didn't want to pay Alex anything. He had taken too much from me. I wanted to keep the marital home and all of the assets that I earned from all of my hard work.

"I understand, Mrs. Davidson, but if the judge rules for joint custody, then you will have to pay Mr. Davidson child support because you make considerably more than he does," stated Attorney Walker.

"I shouldn't be penalized. It's not my fault that he didn't want to work or finish his MBA," I replied.

"Ok, let's review the marital assets and retirement."

"If we divide the negative equity and retirement 401k and IRA, I propose doing a QDRO for $10,000 and you get to keep your retirement going forward," stated Attorney Walker.

"That sounds like an excellent idea," I replied.

We wrapped up and headed downstairs. Mr. Green met us at the elevator and stated that his client wanted to go through mediation. What? What kind of trick was he trying to pull now? This was a final hearing. His attorney was trying to get up to speed. Why bother with mediation? *If I say no, will I be viewed as being uncooperative? If I say yes, will this be a waste of my time? I have to remember the tricks of the enemy. God, what should I do? We opted for mediation to hopefully come to an agreement on some things.*

It was now noon. I hadn't had breakfast and now it was lunch time. Prayer and fasting have paid off. The mediator was an older white man who extended his hand to Attorney Walker. They had a friendly exchange as we walked into the small conference room. Alex's attorney Mr. Green came in with his briefcase tucked under his arm, papers in his hands, and an ink pen between his lips. He laid his things down and said, "May I go to the bathroom first?"

The mediator said, "Yes, we'll get started in a couple of minutes."

A few minutes passed and Alex and Mr. Green entered the room. Mr. Green asked for another chair for the court reporter. The mediator explained that this was a closed session and she was not allowed to be in there. From there I could see the disappointment in Alex's eyes as he whispered to his attorney. He thought he was going to get some testimonial evidence to use in the divorce case. To paint me as an unfit, mentally ill person that didn't deserve custody. The mediator asked us a series of questions and started to recap what he'd heard.

When we get to retirement, my attorney presented the proposal of dividing the debt and retirement and establishing a QDRO. The mediator liked the idea and started jotting down numbers. Alex and Mr. Green were trying hard to catch up. I laughed inside because I already knew what she was referring to. We pulled out all of the documents and went through them one by one to allow the slow learners to catch up. Finally, we were all on the same page in the book. *Can we turn the page?*

We moved on to the most important aspect, custody. Mr. Davidson wanted primary custody, of course. He didn't love Kobe; he was just using him to get paid. Attorney Walker said that Kobe had to live in Dekalb County in order to continue going to the Dekalb School of the Arts. Alex replied, "Yes, and that won't be an issue because I'm moving closer to the school at the end of the month."

This was a major bomb dropped in our laps. His attorney was just as devious as Mr. Davidson for not disclosing this information. I found this rather interesting, since he couldn't afford the place where they were currently living.

The mediator completed his recap and concluded that we had an agreement on two things: assets and who will make the final decision. We left the conference room and headed down the hall to the courtroom. By now it was after 3:00. We passed the court reporter and she indicated to Mr. Davidson that she'd have to get paid for her time. The attorneys walked back to the judge's chambers. The bailiff, court reporter and I struck up a conversation about the championship football game between Alabama and

Clemson. The bailiff was a diehard Alabama fan. Mr. Davidson sat at his table, anti-social as usual.

The attorneys came back. There wasn't an agreement on anything; it was too late in the day to have the judge review the case.

What a waste of time. I should have known better. Why would I expect cooperation from him? And to make matters worse, the judge wanted us to come back tomorrow. I had so much to do at the office. How was I going to explain this to my supervisor JoAnne? We had a major kick-off meeting this week. Alex wouldn't have to worry about child support because I wouldn't have a job.

This process had left me numb. His lies, deceit, and attacks, the stress, pressure and adversity were almost too much to bear. At times, I had felt like a deflated balloon being tossed around as the air continued to be sucked out of me. Other times, it was more like a dog's chew toy and I could feel the teeth sinking into my flesh, picking me up and shaking me until I was barely conscious.

It was just hard to fathom the pain and agony one person could inflict upon another. I had shared my life with this person, loved and trusted this person. I had a family with this person. I thought he had my best interests at heart, but that wasn't the case.

Where would I be without God? He is the source of my strength. He will never leave me nor forsake me. I knew that no matter what it looked like, all things were working for my good. This gave me solace as I prepared to go back to court tomorrow. I would have to carry the divorce baby another day. These were Braxton-Hicks contractions, the fake kind that make you think you are in labor, only to be sent back home. Just like his fake ass that didn't agree with any of the terms, I was sent back home.

Kobe was waiting for me to pick him up from school. My baby, excuse me, my young man, was caught in the middle and was probably punished by his father for loving his mother. You know Alex; he'd tell Kobe you have to love one parent and hate the other parent. He had gone out of his way to make sure that Kobe chose him. Showing interest in his music, Alex was just trying to get paid if Kobe becomes a professional drummer. Of course, Alex strived to be the fun parent, whereas I tried to provide a realistic picture of the world and made sure he studied and went to college.

We headed home and I prepared to call JoAnne and explain that the judge wanted to see us in court tomorrow. She was extremely understanding and said "I'll see you on Wednesday." I was apologetic and she stated, "Life happens." I hung up and went downstairs to prepare dinner and then head to bible study. I needed just a little more Jesus for tomorrow.

I kissed Kobe goodbye and rolled out of the garage. We were studying the movie *War Room* at bible study. "You have to fight, Elizabeth," is what I remembered.

As I headed home, I was more energized until I walked into the house. I called Kobe; no answer. Where could he be? Alex had come to take him to his place. Why? What was he planning now? He'd sell his own soul to get my money. Very sad to say. There's nothing I could do tonight except pray everything goes well tomorrow.

CHAPTER
TWENTY-TWO

MASTER OF
DECEPTION

I didn't sleep well the night before. I just wanted it to be over. My discernment was telling me Alex was gonna try to get Kobe to say he'd prefer to be with Alex when he picked him up while I was a bible study. This was a lie, an act of deception, an act of desperation.

Kobe hadn't left for school yet. My mind was thinking the worst. Had Alex committed the ultimate act of revenge by kidnapping and killing Kobe, instead of potentially paying child support? You hear so many stories of men killing their families when divorce was involved. I checked the phone again and panic set in. I decided to send him a text message and wish him a good day at school; that would help put my mind at ease. I finally saw movement as he headed to school.

Relief came over me, but why was Kobe at home so long? He was going to be late for school. I continued with my prayers and got ready to go to the courthouse.

I texted my attorney, "Can Kobe testify?"

She replied, "Yes, but I'll object."

I breathed a sigh of relief. Just trying to determine all of the angles was like playing a game of chess. I had to be very strategic, since I'm the Queen of my Castle.

Attorney Walker greeted me at the courthouse and we walked to the courtroom. The bailiff was there and we talked about the football game. Mr. Green was there. I thought I should probably know his real name since he will cross examine me. We were waiting, then like the rush of winter, Alex entered the courtroom. The judge came in and we all rose. Soon Mr. Davidson took the stand.

He immediately began with his fabricated story of me trying to kill him and how I should go to jail. No one believed him. He produced a lease agreement for a place closer to the school, one that he couldn't afford because it cost more than the dump, he currently lived in.

Mr. Green asked him some basic questions about his schedule, parenting and finally got to the marital assets. Obviously, he had none, but was quick to point out monies in my account and that I made three times what he earned.

He even produced a letter from Kobe stating that he preferred to live with Alex. He had truly brainwashed my child for the love of money. He just kept going on and on, mostly rambling about nothing. He tried to make it sound like Kobe only stayed with me because Kyle was home for the summer. That was not true. I couldn't wait for my attorney to cross examine him.

CHAPTER

TWENTY-THREE

ROUND 1 OF DIVORCE

SHOWDOWN

This was going to be a long day, as Alex tried to speak like he had a frog in his throat. Did he think this made him seem sympathetic? After several responses, the judge warned Mr. Davidson that he was being too vague or that Mr. Green was leading the witness. I continued writing notes for my attorney.

After I finished relating the events of the day, Mr. Thompson looked over his notes and replied, "That sounds like an exhausting day, Mrs. Davidson."

"It was," I replied, "I thought it was going to be over in a couple of hours. Now he's dragged it out to three days. I just want it to be over, so I can walk away and focus all of my energy on me and the criminal case. They have both been like white water rafting. They started out tranquil and then over the falls you go. You tried to paddle to the shore to get out of danger, but the current was too strong and the water took you in the direction it wanted you to go. You have no control over the time you were in court, the day you appeared in court, or if the case was continued. At times it felt like the raft took on water, but we kept trudging ahead."

I told Mr. Thompson that I tried to take my mind off of things to keep my head from pounding. It felt like it was going to explode. My doctor had told me my blood pressure was out of the normal range. You think? I told her it was just stress-related and it would get back to a normal level. There were just too many competing issues. I was worried about Kobe and his statement that he preferred to stay with his dad, worried that someone at my job knew that I'd been arrested, worried that I could go to jail over my actions, worried that Alex would try to kill me, worried that I could have a criminal record, worried that I could lose everything that I worked for, and worried about what my friends would think if they knew what I was going through. So yes, my blood pressure was a little high.

When I got home, I ate, meditated, prayed, and finished the evening with a hot bath, hoping that would help lower my blood pressure. As soon as my head hit the pillow, it was lights out.

CHAPTER

TWENTY-FOUR

ROUND 2 OF DIVORCE
SHOWDOWN

I woke up, said my prayers, and listened to my inspirational songs. I wasn't hungry, but I grabbed an apple and some trail mix just in case. Two hours could turn into all day. Attorney Walker was ready to question Mr. Davidson. She started with the calendar.

She said, "Mr. Davidson, you stated that Kobe prefers to stay with you. How many days a week does he stay with you?"

"I'm not sure, probably 4-5 days a week," replied Mr. Davidson.

"So, if I showed you the calendar that shows Mrs. Davidson's record of when Kobe was with her, will you be able to produce a similar document?" asked Attorney Walker.

"I don't put a price or time limit on the amount of time I spend with my son," replied Mr. Davidson.

"So, the answer would be no," concluded Attorney Walker. "I'll move onto my next point. You indicated that you were outside the school district and you were moving?"

"Yes, we're moving to 3793 Bobbie Lane and Kobe can walk to school from there," stated Mr. Davidson.

"Do you have a rental agreement?" asked Attorney Walker.

"No, but I expect to have one before the end of the day."

"Well, for now it's inadmissible," replied the judge.

Yes, that felt like an uppercut to Alex's jaw.

"Mr. Davidson, you have referred to the incident that occurred between you and Mrs. Davidson as her trying to kill you. Did you seek medical attention that day?" asked Attorney Walker.

"No," Mr. Davidson replied.

"Isn't it true that you actually tried to hurt Mrs. Davidson by leaning your entire weight on her back?"

"No, that's not true," stated Mr. Davidson.

"What about your use of marijuana? Is this your paraphernalia?" asked Attorney Walker.

"Yes, it was, but I don't use marijuana anymore. I stopped about six months ago."

Well, it seems like Mr. Davidson has an answer for everything. Maybe we should order a drug test to confirm, I thought to myself.

Attorney Walker continued. "Let's talk about your relationship with Mrs. Davidson. Would you consider her a good mother?"

"No, she's petty and manipulative. She doesn't have Kobe's interest at heart."

"Was Mrs. Davidson a good wife?"

"No, she wasn't there for me in the relationship," Mr. Davidson stated.

"Mr. Davidson, isn't it true that Mrs. Davidson helped Kobe with his homework and with getting a tutor?"

"Yes, but she didn't know what she was doing," Mr. Davidson replied.

"I'm not sure if I would be able to explain linear equations. How about you? But Mrs. Davidson was and Kobe received a passing grade. You stated that Mrs. Davidson wasn't a good wife. Were you a good husband?"

"Yes, I was invested in the relationship," Mr. Davidson stated.

"If you were so invested, Mr. Davidson, then why does your wife have text messages from you to another woman? Why were you contacting Suzanne to walk in the mountains when you were still married?"

Mr. Davidson sat there with a confused look on his face.

"You stated Mrs. Davidson wasn't there for you, when obviously you were seeking another relationship outside of the marriage."

"It's not what it appears to be," replied Mr. Davidson.

"Well, it appears to be inappropriate for a married man to reach out to date another woman. Your Honor, we move to dismiss the request for alimony."

Wow, that was a combination punch, a TKO that knocked Mr. Davidson off his feet. He's not sure what to do now. I'm sure he was counting on me paying him like he was some type of kept man that was used to a certain lifestyle. Now he will have to work to live.

Round 2 went to Attorney Walker, but just as I suspected, we'd have to come back because Alex used up all of the time saying absolutely nothing. The judge booked us for two weeks out. *Great, more time to formulate our strategy.* I headed out with Attorney Walker. Next time, I'll be on the stand. I can assure you that my testimony will not take a total of four hours. I'm getting ready for Round 3.

CHAPTER
TWENTY-FIVE

ROUND 3 OF DIVORCE
SHOWDOWN

I immediately contacted my prayer warriors. We were at war and I needed some reliable soldiers. I had to be prepared. I worked on gathering more evidence: text messages to show my interactions with Kobe, school schedules, report cards and anything to show that I'm involved in my son's life; a calendar showing the days Kobe was with me, medical history and ID cards. I pulled together bank account information showing that I paid for home repairs, and of course, the text messages showing Alex's infidelity with Suzanne. That should serve as the final knockout punch. Evidence of marijuana use should keep Alex down for the 10-count.

Attorney Walker reached out to me for a pre-court conference to make sure we hit all of the main points for proving I was the parent that should retain full custody.

This had been a long-drawn-out process. Alex's first attorney dropped him as a client which delayed it. I wish I could have heard their interactions. He probably talked to her with disdain.

But now here we are. Let's get ready to rumble. We walked into the courtroom and had a seat at the table. The bailiff and Attorney Walker exchanged pleasantries and started talking about the Alabama team. I joined in the conversation.

Mr. Davidson walked in with his attorney a few minutes before the judge entered. I was sworn in and took the stand. I was wearing one of my usual court outfits, black sweater and skirt with my black boots; I was looking smart, sophisticated, and stylish. Attorney Walker was ready to start with the questions.

"Mrs. Davidson, can you please explain your relationship with your son, Kobe?"

"Yes, we have a very close relationship. I'm involved with every aspect of his life, from schooling, to his friends, to his personal welfare. He loves me. And I love him. I help him with his homework. I attend all of his games, performances, and open house. I take him to tutoring and drum lessons, as well as paying for them."

"Is it safe to say that you were primarily responsible for his education?" asked Attorney Walker.

"Yes, I am responsible for his education," I replied.

"And how much time do you spend with him?"

"I take him to school and pick him up. We go home, so I spend most of the time with him, except when he's in school."

"How does Mr. Davidson interact with your son?" asked Attorney Walker.

"His work schedule doesn't permit much time for him to spend with Kobe. He may spend Sunday at home in front of the TV."

"Mrs. Davidson, what about medical decisions?"

"I carried all four of us on my medical plan until 2012 when Mr. Davidson got coverage through his employer. Now I cover me and the boys. I take Kobe for his medical, dental, and vision appointments. I'm a good mom and Kobe wants to stay with me, but he can visit his dad."

"Let's talk about your relationship with Mr. Davidson. You have been married for 22 years?"

"Yes, that's correct, but about seven years ago, he checked out of the marriage. It lacked regular intimacy. He ignored some of my sexual advances. Maybe he was having an affair then, I'm not sure. He told me he wanted a divorce but then asked if he could stay in the house because he didn't have money to move out. He also stopped wearing his wedding ring."

"Mrs. Davidson, you mentioned that you thought there was infidelity in the marriage. What made you think that?"

"I saw a text message between Mr. Davidson and someone named Suzanne."

"Your Honor, please see exhibit 1A. Mrs. Davidson, can you read the text?"

"Yes, 'Suzanne, I want to walk through the Kennesaw mountains with you.' I also saw a letter that he wrote to a female telling her that he liked her vibe and that he had two sons and was ready to make a move. I made a copy of it, but he removed it from my briefcase."

Alex's attorney objected, "Hearsay."

"Mrs. Davidson, did Mr. Davidson contribute to the household?"

"No, Mr. Davidson didn't have a real job until he started working for State Farm. He was spending his time and money on smoking marijuana."

"Your Honor, exhibit 2A," Attorney Walker said. Then to me, she said, "Can you describe what this is?"

"Yes, it's a photo of Mr. Davidson's marijuana bag and tools."

"Did he smoke on a regular basis?" asked Attorney Walker.

"Yes, every day. He was out of control," I stated.

"Did he have a prescription?"

"No, not that I'm aware of."

"One last question, do you consider yourself a good mother?"

"Yes," I replied.

"Nothing further, Your Honor."

Now I guessed it was time for me to be cross-examined Alex's attorney. I refer to him as Mr. Green because I didn't know his real name and he looked new to the court system, like he was trying to figure things out as he went along.

"Hello, Mrs. Davidson," said Mr. Green. "How long have you been married to Mr. Davidson?"

"It has been 22 years. We were married in 1992."

"Did you take care of the household expenses?" asked Mr. Green.

"Yes, because Mr. Davidson didn't have a regular full-time job for over ten years until he got hired by State Farm in 2013," I replied.

"Did you have a joint account with Mr. Davidson?" Mr. Green asked.

"No, but he had access to my account to transfer monies into his account."

I could see Alex advising his attorney to present my banking information as if he was entitled to monies from my account. I could see him pointing at the document to ask me about a certain line item.

Mr. Green handed me my bank statement and said, "Mrs. Davidson, your bank statement shows a balance of $35,000. Can you please explain where the money came from?"

"Yes, some of it was from my son Kyle to pay for his car that I financed. And the rest was the insurance money that I received when our house was broken into and I financed the repairs. Mr. Davidson didn't take care of anything around the house or anything in the house."

"What about the payment for $5000, Mrs. Davidson?"

"That was to pay for my grandmother's funeral," I replied.

"Mrs. Davidson, I show that you have a health savings account."

"Yes, I do."

"Your Honor, Mr. Davidson is requesting that Mrs. Davidson cover his medical expenses because he is entitled to monies in the HSA account."

"Mr. Davidson is enrolled in a medical plan with HRA and therefore isn't eligible to receive monies from an HSA. It's an IRS restriction," I explained.

"Are you an expert for how the health savings account works?" asked the judge.

"Your Honor, Mrs. Davidson works in human resources and is familiar with how benefits, including health savings accounts work," stated Attorney Walker.

"No further questions, Your Honor," stated Mr. Green.

As I stepped off the stand, I felt pretty confident that I was able to explain all of the monies in my account. I knew he was going to focus on the dollars so I had receipts for everything. Out of the corner of my eye I saw Mr. Green pack up his papers into an oversized briefcase. You know, the kind you get from your granddad. He looked real out of place and Mr. Davidson had that shriveled up prune look, as if he smelled something disgusting, like he was constipated with shit clogging his colon, like bitterness was the only emotion he could display.

I asked Attorney Walker, "What are the next steps?"

"We'll have to wait until the judge rules. It will probably take 1-2 weeks."

"Will we have to come back to court?" I asked.

"No, the judge will send her decision."

I exited the courthouse feeling like Round 3 may have been a draw. Yeah, I was able to prove where all the money came from, except $5000, but the judge questioned me on the Health Savings Account. She didn't think I was an expert on the matter, but didn't have enough experience to rule in Mr. Davidson's favor.

I thanked God that it was over and tried to take my mind off things. What a way to start off the New Year, still tied to someone that has managed to drag the process out for months. Now all I could do was wait and pray. "Dear Heavenly Father, I thank you for this day and ask that I find favor with the judge as she reviews my case. In Jesus name, Amen."

CHAPTER

TWENTY-SIX

THE DECISION

About a week after going to court, Attorney Walker gave me a call and indicated that the judge had rendered a decision.

"I'm going to email you the decision and please call me if you have any questions," Attorney Walker said.

I immediately logged into my email account and opened up the documents. I was reading through it and tears were welling up in my eyes. I could barely breathe. We had joint custody of Kobe. I had final say over medical, religion and education. I kept reading and found that I was mandated to pay Mr. Davidson $600 per month for child support until Kobe graduated. WHAT? That meant paying him for the next four years. How was this possible? Why was I asked to pay him child support when we have joint custody?

I kept reading and found that the amount was modified based on the time that Kobe was scheduled to spend with me. I started sobbing profusely. Alex was not going to use the money to take care of Kobe, he was going to use it to take care of himself. He couldn't afford to live where he moved, so $600 was a huge offset to help him keep a roof over his head.

I kept reading. The schedule was defined by which days Kobe was supposed to be with me and days he was with Alex. I didn't realize how strict this was going to be. Kobe was 14 and should be able to determine which parent he wanted to stay with on which day. One glimmer of hope was that the schedule could be modified if Alex agreed, which would undoubtedly never happen.

I pulled up the second document, the divorce decree. I always find it interesting the value that a piece of paper has over your life; a birth certificate, a high school diploma, a college degree, a marriage license, and now a divorce decree. I read each page carefully. And then I cried again. The judge had ordered me to pay Mr. Davidson $5,000. He didn't deserve another penny from me.

What else was I required to do? The judge wanted me to give Mr. Davidson half of my HSA account. This was so unfair when I covered all of his medical expenses when he was on my insurance. What else was I required to do? I was sure it would have something to do with me paying more to Mr. Davidson. I was right. Now, I was ordered to give him monies from one of my 401k plans. He didn't deserve what I've worked so hard for. I was so upset I could hardly think. *Maybe there's a way to appeal this decision*, I thought. *Let me call Attorney Walker.*

"Hi Attorney Walker, I've received the divorce decree and have some questions regarding the child support payment."

"Hello, Ms. Davidson. As you recall, I mentioned that in Georgia, the parent that makes the most income will be ordered to pay child support."

"Is there anything, anything we can do to change this?" I asked.

"Unfortunately, the divorce decree and child support are final."

The word *final* kept ringing in my ears. This was insane. I felt like I was totally taken advantage of, that in the end there was no way around my paying Alex. I prayed, "Lord, enlarge my territory to not feel the $600 dollars from my paycheck."

I thought I should probably let Mr. Thompson know that the divorce was final. As I called his office, I really didn't have the energy for an impromptu session, so I was relieved when I get his voicemail.

At the beep, I left him the following message: "Hello, Mr. Thompson. This is Mrs. Davidson. I mean Ms. Davidson. It's gonna take me a minute to get used to saying it. I wanted to let you know that the divorce is final and I'd like to have some time to process all of this before having another session. Can I call to schedule a session in a couple of months?"

I hung up the phone and just sat there gathering my thoughts. I was so stuck on *final* that I didn't even notice the phone vibrating.

Mr. Thompson had called me back. He said, "Hi Ms. Davidson, just call our office when you're ready to schedule your next appointment. In the meantime, I want you to continue to write. It will be therapeutic to get your thoughts and feelings out. This will help you get used to your new status. You should be proud of all that you have accomplished and divorce is not the end of the world. Ok, we'll talk soon..."

www.ingramcontent.com/pod-product-compliance
Lightning Source LLC
Chambersburg PA
CBHW020437180626
46812CB00003B/1274